WARREN LANE

ANDREW DIAMOND

Published by Stolen Time Press, Charlottesville, VA
http://www.stolentimepress.com

May, 2015 – First Edition

ISBN: 978-0-9963507-0-9

For Anne Garrison

All those years ago, when nothing was going right in my life, you listened patiently to my complaints and helped me through to better days. On your final birthday, when we all said what we valued most in you, your daughter spoke for everyone when she described how supportive and encouraging you were. The world is poorer without you in it, but the seeds you nurtured in the ones you loved are still growing, and your generosity and your faith in us continue to bear fruit.

Chapter 1

Will Moore sat in a lounge chair by the hotel pool in his Bermuda shorts and white polo shirt, browsing through photos of escorts on his phone. The dark-haired one reminded him of his wife when she was young. He instinctively looked to her eyes in search of the deep feeling and sharp intelligence of the woman he loved. But these eyes were empty, and everything about the photo looked fake, from the blow-dried hair to the over-done make-up to the glossy, slightly parted lips that promised pleasure.

Will put the phone down and thought, *Why am I looking at her? I can have her at home. And she's better now than she was at that age.*

He looked out toward the broad, extravagant pool where the mothers and fathers played with their children. In winter, there would be hundreds of people here, but May was the beginning of the slow season in Miami, and there were no more than twenty guests on the deck this morning. It was quiet enough to hear the breeze in the palms and the waves breaking beyond the bushes.

At fifty, Will looked like an inflated version of himself at thirty. The weight he had put on through years of indulgence in beef and alcohol was evenly distributed throughout his body, and he carried it well. His brown hair showed no trace of grey. His skin was stretched smooth across his broad face, which was red from the South Florida heat. He had the healthy, vigorous look of a man who enjoyed life, and the easy confidence of a man accustomed to getting what he wants.

He thought back to the young woman he had met at the party a few nights before, with the blonde hair and the clear blue eyes, the quick smile and the easy, open manner. She was one of the models hired to mix with the guests; but her lithe, athletic figure, her dancer's grace and upright posture made her stand out from the others, who looked skinny and underfed. She told him over a glass of wine that she had trained in ballet as a teenager and then quit when the pressure to be perfect took all the joy out of it. She liked to joke and flirt. She was simple and direct. She was in every way the opposite of his wife, whose life was all interior. Too bad he blew his chance with her.

They had shared a cab back to the hotel after the party and had a drink at the bar. At the end of the evening, when she said good-bye as she left the elevator, her backward glance lingered just a split second too long, and he knew he had an opportunity.

He ran into her in the lobby the next night, after his dinner plans fell through. Did she have plans? No. He took her to a restaurant and they went through two bottles of expensive wine. He told her about his business, importing high-end furniture and art from Asia. She told him about modeling and her life in New York.

She was lively, open and expressive, and he marveled at how willingly she went along with his plan, drinking all the wine he offered, like Gretel readying herself for the witch's pleasure. She was clearly intelligent. She knew where this was going. But she seemed to him a little reckless. Perhaps a little self-destructive. He kept refilling her glass before she could empty it.

In the cab back to the hotel, she began to slouch, and her head bobbed whenever the car hit a bump. In the elevator, she leaned heavily against the wall. When the doors opened on the ninth floor, Will held her just above the elbow to steady her. His grip was almost tight enough to bruise. At the end of the hallway, she wavered on her feet as he slid the magnetic key card into the lock. She said in a pathetic voice, "I drank too much, Will. I don't feel good."

Will steered her to bed and sat her down. He knelt and removed her shoes. Then he went into the bathroom and raised the toilet seat and dropped a towel on the floor. A few seconds later, she stumbled in with her hand over her mouth, the vomit pushing through her fingers as she leaned toward the toilet.

Will left the bathroom without a word. She stayed on her knees for several minutes, vomiting and cleaning up after herself. When she returned to the room, Will was sitting on the couch. He watched in silence as she walked to the side of the bed. She looked at him sadly and began to pull down the strap of her dress.

Will shook his head. "Don't do that."

"No?"

"No. Get some sleep."

She lay on top of the covers, and Will filled a glass of water in the bathroom. When he set it on the nightstand beside her, he asked, "Do you feel better?"

"The room's not spinning anymore."

He turned out the lamp next to the bed.

When she awoke sweating in the middle of the night, Will was asleep on the couch, still fully dressed. At 8:00 a.m., he was sitting by her side in a fresh suit of clothes, gently rubbing her shoulder. "I hope you feel better," he said. "I'm sorry about last night. That was my fault."

That was yesterday morning. He had thought of her often since then. If she had come from the agency, he might have made her go through with it. But then, if she had come from the agency, he would not have had to get her drunk. She would have been happy to collect whatever her share of the $1500 fee was. Will tried to tally up how much his little habit had cost him over the past twelve months, but he couldn't even remember how many cities he had visited in that time.

A year and half earlier, he was surprised when his accountant, Arnie, confronted him about his escapades. Arnie's disapproving mention of *your little call girls* rankled him. An accountant, of all people, should see the sense of negotiating a fee for a service. It was so much neater than the unpredictable and ongoing expenses of a real relationship.

But Arnie had pulled him aside and said, "What's going on, Will? You used to go to Asia every six or eight weeks. Now you're there ten or fifteen days out of every month. Or you're in New York, or Miami, or Vegas. Why?"

"It's business," Will explained.

"You can't keep giving me these expense reports, flying first class and staying in suites in five-star hotels," Arnie said. "You can't keep charging dinners for half a dozen people with wine at two-hundred dollars a bottle."

"Relax," said Will.

"Uh-uh," said Arnie. "Your travel and entertainment expenses are way too high. The IRS won't allow it. We're already cash-poor from all the money you took out of the company to put into that trust. We could have kept the stores open in Portland and Seattle if you weren't skimming off all the profits. It's cash flow that's killing us."

"It's my company," Will said.

"And that's why you should be concerned," Arnie said. "If we hit two bad months in a row, we'll be leaning hard on our credit line. I don't want to borrow to finance your extravagance."

"OK, Arnie, I get it. You don't need to lecture me."

"Sorry, Will, but I think I *do* need to lecture you. You're running off the rails here. You built this company by being frugal and making wise choices. When you had your fun, you did it on the cheap. Now you're getting to be the fat old lion that lives for the spoils more than the hunt." Arnie lowered his voice and said sternly, "I read the credit card statements every month. Your personal ones too. If I see one of your little call girls show up on a company card, I'm not paying it."

"Do you think I'm that stupid?" Will started to turn away, but Arnie caught his arm.

"I don't know, Will." Arnie's voice was serious. "I'm just trying to bring you back on track. You have to tone it down. Get back to being the person who built this business."

Will considered his words. Finally, he said, "I'll keep my eyes open for opportunities. We can bring in more revenue."

Arnie frowned. "That's not the answer I wanted to hear, Will. It's not just the cash flow I'm worried about."

Will found his new revenue stream, and he told himself as he watched the palms swaying in the breeze that he should have spent some of that cash on a professional instead of wasting his time with the blonde-haired girl. Now he was sitting by the pool because he knew she was still in the hotel. She ran in the mornings then went to the beach for a swim. Wouldn't it be nice if she walked by and he got another chance?

But it was too hot, even in the shade, and he was about to go in when he saw her coming toward him. She wore a blue bikini beneath a see-through white wrap. Her hair was tied in a ponytail, and her face was flushed and covered with beads of sweat from the run she had just finished.

There was that smile again. That bright, lovely smile. "Hi, Will."

"Hey Ella. How far did you run?"

"Eight miles. I have to cool down."

"You want a drink?"

"No alcohol," she said.

"No, something cool. The waiter is on his way over."

9

"Maybe a daiquiri," she said. "Without the rum."

Will ordered the drink, while Ella fanned herself with her hand and watched the children in the pool.

"When's your next shoot?" Will asked.

"In two days."

"Mmm. Too bad I'll miss it."

"When do you leave?" Ella asked.

"Tomorrow. Late morning."

They were quiet for a moment, then Ella began, "Will..."

His phone rang. He looked at the name on the screen, and then held up his finger and said, "Just a minute. I have to take this. Hello?"

His eyes narrowed and his body tensed as he listened. "What do you mean, stuck in customs? How could it be stuck?" He paused and listened. "It was just random? Well, where is it?" Pause. "OK, the X-ray is broken. Is it in the machine?" He listened again. "Are they going to open the container?" Pause. "Well goddammit, what *do* you know?" He let out a sigh as the person on the other end spoke, then he said with frustration and a tinge of fear, "You call me as soon as something happens."

When he hung up, he looked pale and his breathing was fast and shallow. He stood up and ran his fingers through his hair, then, looking a little dizzy, he sat back down.

"You OK, Will?" Ella asked.

"No."

"What's the matter?"

"Business. Bad business." His chest tightened, he struggled to breathe, and his face looked ashen.

"Oh my God, Will! Are you having a heart attack?"

"No. Shut up. Don't make a scene."

"You need an ambulance."

Will looked at her sternly and said in the calmest voice he could muster, "No ambulance. No scene. Just get me a cab."

They stood and walked into the hotel, her arm steadying him as he had steadied her two nights before. She reminded him to breathe deeply as they passed slowly through the lobby.

She got him into a cab in the hotel drive, and they went to the hospital. Ella held his phone and wallet while the doctors examined him and ordered tests. After two hours, she peeked in on him as he sat on the edge of an examination table in a white paper robe.

The doctor said, "Your pulse is strong and your heart sounds fine, but your blood pressure and your cholesterol are high." He looked at Will's chart. "You say there's no history of heart disease on your mother's side. What about your father's side?"

"I never met my father," Will said.

"Have you ever had an anxiety attack?" the doctor asked.

"Ha! I'm not an anxious person," Will said.

"Are you under stress at work?"

"I had a scare today."

"That's when the tightness and breathing problems started?"

"Yeah."

"Will," said Ella. "Someone called you twice. I didn't answer."

"Can I have the phone?" Will asked. He went into the hall and made a call. Ella heard him say, "So it's through? Why didn't you call me?" Pause. "Oh, right. You did. I didn't have the phone with me. Sorry." He let out a long breath. "Shit!"

He returned to the room looking more relaxed. "Come on," he said to Ella. "Let's get out of here." He removed the hospital gown and put his shirt on.

"Mr. Moore," said the doctor, "I think you should have more tests. I don't think you had a cardiac event, but you are at risk."

"Doc, I'm fine." He turned to Ella and said, "Come on, let's go."

"Do you want anything for the anxiety?" the doctor asked.

"Scotch," said Will.

They took a cab back to the hotel. Will spent most of the drive quietly looking out the window. He was breathing easily, though he looked tired. From the driveway to his room, Ella walked with her arm through his. He didn't need help at this point, but he enjoyed her touch. She left him on the couch in his room, where he stared blankly at the wall, rubbing the hint of stubble on his chin.

"I hope you feel better," she said.

"Hmm? Oh. Thanks for coming with me. Sorry to ruin your day."

"You didn't ruin it. Are you sure you'll be OK?"

"I'll be fine," Will said.

When she left, he stretched out on the couch and thought about how to get out of this business he was in. He fell asleep after half an hour and woke again at 5:00 p.m. when Ella knocked on his door. She was wearing the same bikini and wrap. Her cheeks were a little sunburned and she had sand on her calves and feet.

She presented him with a bottle of Scotch and said, "For your anxiety."

"For my pleasure," said Will. "Come in."

Ella walked to the balcony door, and Will unwrapped the two glasses on the mini-fridge. "Would you like some?" he asked.

Ella squinted and held her hand in front of her eye, her thumb and forefinger half an inch apart. Will poured a tall glass for himself and a shot for her. He sat on the couch and she sat next to him, turning sideways and pointing her knees toward him as he handed her the glass. They made a toast. "To joy," Will said.

"To your health," said Ella. She took a sip and made an unpleasant face. She drank the remainder in a single gulp, and then said, "So what was that all about?"

"You don't want to know," Will said.

"Do you always get so wrapped up in work?"

"Let's talk about something else."

With a mischievous smile, she put her finger in the open collar of his shirt and rubbed the hair beneath his collarbone.

"Am I getting under your skin, Will?"

"You're... What are you doing?"

"What do you want me to do?"

He looked at her and wondered, *Is she a prostitute?*

She stood up and removed the wrap around her bikini.

If she's not, he thought, *she's racing toward trouble.*

Ella said in a teasing, condescending voice, "Does the big bad customs man scare you?"

She poured herself another shot of Scotch and said in a flirtatious tone of mock-annoyance, "I'm bored, and the straps of my top are digging into my skin."

She sat on the couch again, closer to him this time, so the straps were within his reach. When he hesitated, she said, "Are you scared, Will? I didn't take you for the hesitant type."

In a minute, she was undressed and undressing him. She took his hand and pulled him from the couch to the bed. Then she turned and opened the sliding glass doors. She walked onto the balcony, leaned against the rail and looked out over the pool, the dark green palms and the turquoise water of the Atlantic. Her behind was a little whiter than the rest of her.

"What the hell are you doing?" Will said. "It's still daylight. People will see you!"

"Look at this view, Will. I love the color of the sea."

"Get in here!" Will demanded.

Ella turned to face him and said flatly, "Come out and get me."

"Are you crazy? You're going to get us thrown out of here."

She leaned back against the railing and smiled. "You're leaving tomorrow anyway. Come join me. The air is wonderful."

Will put on his shorts and stormed onto the balcony. He grabbed her by the arm, pulled her back into the room, and slid the glass door shut with almost enough force to break it.

Ella smiled at him. "You're dressed again. Now we'll have to start all over. And look at you shake. Are you that angry?"

"You fucking lunatic! I know people in this hotel. They know me. You can't behave like that."

"You're not going to let me get away with this, are you Will?"

He pushed her to the bed. She reclined onto her elbows and smiled and said, "Don't break me, Will."

A short time later, they were lying side by side. Will was on his back. Ella was on her side, her index finger tracing circles in the hair on his chest.

Will said, "You're crazy, you know that?"

"I know. You are too. I was worried for a while you might have a real heart attack, the way you were going at it."

"You got me all wound up," said Will.

"It's not hard to do," said Ella.

"I like you," Will said.

"Mmm. I like you too." She plucked a hair from his chest.

"Ow! What was that for?"

"For letting your guard down."

She turned onto her stomach and propped herself on her elbows. "Will. You said the other night you like a woman's body. Every part of her body." She rolled onto her back and said, "Show me what you like."

Will sat up and looked at her.

"Go ahead," she said. "Take your time, and show me all the things you like."

"Really?"

"Yeah. I got what I wanted. Now it's your turn."

This comment, more than anything she had done or said, caught him off guard. He thought he had just gotten what he wanted. He thought that *was* his turn. Who was playing whom in this little game?

Did it matter? She had invited him in for more.

Chapter 2

That was how the affair began, and Will thought it would end there in Miami. But she told him she would be in Los Angeles the following month for a series of photo shoots. Will lived in Santa Barbara and had plenty of excuses to travel to LA, where his company maintained an office, a warehouse, and a showroom.

He told her to rent a car and pick a nice hotel. "Put it on your card, and I'll pay the bill."

When he first saw her in LA, he was struck again by the brightness of her presence. Her clear eyes, clear skin, clear voice, her openness and her ready smile brought youth and light into his day. But she was on her way down, he could tell. In bed, she was wild in a way that none of his prostitutes could fake, as if she were willing to destroy herself all at once, in a single act.

If he had had soul enough to care for her, he would have been alarmed. He would have tried to help. But he was having too much fun, and he didn't expect his young prize to be around much longer. LA had plenty of men with eyes out for women for like her.

The last time they were together in the hotel in Los Angeles, she looked tired and worn, and she kept sniffling. After sex, they watched TV in the hotel bed while she held on to him. He looked at all her shopping bags full of new clothing and tried to calculate in his head how much it would cost him to pay off that credit card bill. He made a guess and divided the figure by the number of times they had sex. She was cheaper than some of his call girls.

When he got up to leave, she said, "Please don't go."

"I'm spent for today," he said. "I couldn't go again if I wanted to."

"I don't mean that. I just mean... we could order in some food. I don't want to go out, and I don't want to be alone." Her eyes were a little bloodshot and red around the rims.

She's not as pretty when she looks sick, Will thought. *I don't like her when she looks like that.* He started to put on his clothes.

"I haven't slept in two days," she said. "I'm fucking up, Will. I have to get out of LA."

"I have a house in Goleta," he said as put on his shirt. The house was one of the secrets he kept from his wife. He stored some valuable furniture there, and kept the place handy for dalliances when he couldn't get out of town. "If you need a retreat, you're welcome to it."

"Send me the address," she said.

He didn't think she'd take him up on it, but she called him on her way up from LA a few days later. He met her in front of the house, and she wouldn't get out of the little convertible Mustang she had rented, so he got in and they talked.

In LA, she said, she was doing a lot of cocaine. "I just... I just hooked up with the wrong people." Her eyes kept drooping as if she might nod off. "I wouldn't touch it in New York, because I hate what it does to people. It brings out the worst in everyone. Even me. I start acting like my sister. I can't go back there."

Will gave her the key to the house. He left her alone, and she spent much of the next three days sleeping. When he stopped by the house on the fourth day, she was just returning from a run. Her glow and her smile were back.

In the kitchen, she reminded him that he'd promised to pay her credit card bill. "I'll pay it," he said.

She hesitated then said, "I have three cards."

"OK," Will said.

"Two of them are maxed out. And I'm down to, like, two hundred bucks on the third. Do you think you can pay one of them?"

"Send me the bills," Will said. "I'll pay them."

He didn't ask for sex that day. He wanted to give her another day to recover. As he drove back to his office, he thought, *I'll wait a while before I pay those bills. If she's really down to two hundred bucks, she can't go anywhere.*

After a couple of days, Ella understood he was stalling. She thought her generosity in bed might inspire him to pay, but it only made him want to keep her around longer. By her seventh day in the house, she resented him and felt trapped. She had enough gas in the car to get back to LA, but things there would be worse. Her job was gone. She had missed four days of shooting and hadn't returned her agent's calls. The only thing waiting for her in LA was her troubled group of friends and their cocaine.

Her eighth day in the house was the first day of summer. She called her sister and asked her to buy a plane ticket back to New York.

"Why can't you buy it yourself?" her sister asked.

"Because, Anna, I just don't have any money right now."

"Oh, God, what the hell did you do?" Anna asked. "Did you get yourself fired?"

"I... I don't know. I kind of drifted away. I started seeing this guy in LA. His friends were all, like... They were a mess. None of them ever slept."

"So you're in LA?"

"Goleta, actually."

"What are you doing there?"

Ella was silent.

"Well?" her sister demanded. "Are you going to answer?"

"I'm sorry," is all Ella could say.

"So you're seeing some guy in Goleta? Are you pregnant?"

"No."

"Are you in danger?"

"No."

Her sister let out a long sigh. "I can't tell you how much it pisses me off to see all the ways you fuck up."

"You don't have to tell me," Ella said. "I know, OK? I know I fucked up. Will you help me?"

Her sister sighed again, as if to rub it in. "OK. Santa Barbara to New York?"

"Yes."

"Any particular day?"

"As soon as you can."

"OK," said Anna. "I'll call you back."

Anna called back later that afternoon. "I got you on an afternoon flight in three days."

"Thank you," Ella said. "Thank you."

"You'll have to find your own way from the airport."

"Thank you," Ella said again.

"You owe me," said Anna.

"I know."

Once again, her spirit was light. Will noticed it immediately when he visited that afternoon. He found her irresistible when she was bright and happy, and he couldn't wait to have sex with her. At first she demurred. She was done with him and wanted to be polite about it.

But he was persistent and so blinded by desire he couldn't see how far apart they were in their feelings for each other. Finally, she agreed. She would express in this one final act all her hatred for him. Her contempt for him only grew when she saw how excited he was. He trembled, as he had that first time in Miami.

She pushed him down angrily, leaning against his throat as she climbed on top. She gave free reign to her hatred, and in doing so, she tapped into a deep well of frustration with her life and herself. It flowed out freely and uncontrollably. She was aggressive, rough, rude, and abusive. The act of love looked like an act of violence. Will found this a tremendous turn-on, and to her surprise, so did she.

All she could think about after he left was how she wanted to do it again, and this scared her. She was physically and emotionally wide open, ready to receive the person who would cross her path in just a few days. The one she might otherwise have turned away from.

Chapter 3

Susan Moore stood in her bedroom wearing only a bra and underpants on that first shining day of summer. Her dark-brown hair, still damp from the shower, fell just past her shoulders. Her sharp, dark eyes instantly conveyed a commanding intelligence. Her chest and hips were full and soft, the flesh bulging just slightly around the top of her underwear and the side straps of her bra. Outside the window of the high-ceilinged room, down the hill, past the palms and the terra cotta rooftops of Santa Barbara, a tiny white sail glided silently across the glistening Pacific.

On her way to the closet, Susan stopped and picked up the wedding photo from the dresser. She and Will were thinner then. She remembered the moment the photo was taken, and how genuinely she meant that smile.

Will had found her at just the right time in her life; or perhaps, as she now thought, just the wrong time. Fifteen years ago, in the weeks before her parents' accident, she was waiting tables at The Evening Star in Los Angeles. Will had seen her there before, but he felt no particular interest in her until she waited on him. When she approached his table that evening, he thought, *Ah, the unsmiling one.* She was quiet and introverted, and had the placid, slightly distant expression of a daydreamer.

When she introduced herself and described the day's specials, she stood with her shoulders square to him, looking directly into his face with an open, unguarded expression. Behind her eyes was a deep sea of feeling and imagination. Part of her was somewhere else. The dark, lively eyes and the direct simplicity of her manner drew him in like a whispering voice. When she spoke, he felt as if they were the only two people in the room.

Throughout the meal, Will watched her come and go among the tables. Her face occasionally showed hints of emotion that had nothing to do with what was going on around her. *She's responding to her thoughts,* Will realized. *And there's a lot going on in there.*

When she waited on him again two weeks later, it was clear she didn't remember him. He tried without success to engage her in conversation, then watched with jealousy as a huge smile spread across her face in response to a little whisper from the bartender.

Her face still bore a trace of that smile when she brought his check a minute later. The sight of her so far removed from his feelings of envy and desire filled him with a sense of hopelessness. She asked if everything was OK.

"Oh. Yeah. Everything was fine," he said, though she could see it wasn't.

He signed the check, adding a generous tip, and then got up to leave. Two steps from the table, he felt a touch on his shoulder, and turned to see her looking up at him with an expression of gratitude.

"Thank you," she said.

The powerful swelling he felt in his chest in response to this recognition was as disconcerting as it was uplifting. His heart was not the organ that normally responded to women.

A few days later, she left LA and returned to San Diego to care for her parents, who had barely survived a collision on the freeway. She didn't show up for the beginning of her graduate program, and when she failed to return the university's calls, she forfeited her scholarship and the future she had planned.

When her father left the hospital with a cane, his mouth hung slightly open. The words that had once come easily to the avid reader and bookstore owner now eluded him, and he had trouble making sense of simple newspaper articles. In the middle of a sentence, he would sometimes stop abruptly, searching silently for the next word before giving up in frustration and dismay. Over time, he talked less and less.

Her mother, who bore the brunt of the impact, was in and out of the hospital for eight months before pneumonia finally took her. Susan was at her bedside with her father when he pointed to the oxygen tubes in her nose and said with unusual clarity, "Don't let me go like that."

Those words unnerved her. Where was he going? He was all she had left. But after losing his words and his books and his wife, he found less and less to draw him out of bed each day. Susan knew he was giving up, but she couldn't bring herself to admit it. Gentle as he was, he was the model of strength in her life. If death took him by force, there was no shame in that. But if he gave in willingly, why should anyone continue? He died less than a month after her mother.

She never quite got over the abandonment and betrayal she felt at his death. Mentally and emotionally, she felt as if she had been stripped down to nothing, and she would have to rebuild her life and herself from the ground up. But she had no ground to build on, except the wound of her loss.

And so, as an oyster builds a pearl around the irritating grain of sand, she wrapped layer upon layer of defenses around her wound. Over the years, a strong mind, a quiet pride, emotional depth and a natural reserve gave the pearl its luster, and men and women alike admired her. Now, at forty, she was just reaching the peak of her beauty. A younger face could not express the depth of her character.

She didn't remember meeting Will at the restaurant. In her telling of the story, she first saw him in LA a little more than a year after her parents' death. She watched from the window of a coffee shop as two men argued over a parking space. It looked like the larger man was going to hit the smaller one when Will strolled casually into the scene and said something she couldn't hear.

The big man replied to Will with some menacing words, and the little one took the opportunity to get away. Will stood his ground and kept talking, in a casual, almost playful way, and gradually the big man relaxed. In a minute, they were joking with each other.

When Susan returned to the bookstore where she worked, she replayed the scene in her mind, trying to fill in the words she couldn't hear. In those days, she had a vague, persistent fear that some new disaster was always just around the corner. The little scene in front of the coffee shop impressed her because Will had intentionally walked into a dangerous situation and then took control of it. She kept asking herself, *How can a person approach the world that way?* But she couldn't answer that question.

Two weeks later, Will walked into the bookstore. She recognized him right away, and watched from the register as he browsed the business section. Her curiosity overcame her shyness, drawing her silently forward until she stood beside him.

When he turned to find the eyes from The Evening Star looking up at him, the expression of surprise on his face caused her to say, "I'm sorry. I didn't mean to sneak up on you."

She wondered as his look of surprise melted into recognition: *Do you know me?*

"Can I help you find something?" she asked.

He had already found the book he came for, and he watched her quietly as she rang up the purchase. She kept her eyes on the register and didn't look up at him until the sale was complete, although she could tell he was admiring her. As she folded the top of the paper bag and handed it to him, she finally raised her eyes to his and looked at him with the same open, unselfconscious expression that had enchanted him twice before.

Her eyes took in everything, feeding the mind that churned visibly beneath, and he could not help falling into them as they studied him. But her face showed nothing of what she felt. He wanted to say something, but he couldn't find the words.

Then she startled him with a simple question. "Are you going to ask me out?"

If she had asked this with a smile, with a hint of excitement or annoyance, he could have gauged his chances right away. But she asked it as a simple matter-of-fact inquiry, as if she just wanted to know, *Am I reading you right?*

"Because if you are," she said at last, "I'll say yes." Her brow softened. The flesh on her cheeks moved upward almost imperceptibly as the hint of a smile appeared on her lips. Beguiled by these little changes that transformed her, he struggled at first to speak, and then stammered, "Would you like... Would you like to go to dinner?"

She answered softly, "Yes."

At dinner that night, she asked him about the incident in front of the coffee shop. Will didn't remember it until she fed him some details.

"Oh, that," he said, with a dismissive wave. "I don't know what that guy's problem was."

"Why did you get involved?" Susan asked.

"I thought he was going to put his fist through that little guy's face."

"So you volunteered your own face? You don't mind getting hit?"

"Oh, no," Will said. "I do mind getting hit."

"What did you say to him?"

"I asked him if it was really worth getting that upset over a parking space. He kind of looked at me and sized me up, like he was

25

wondering if he should hit me. I could see he didn't really want to take on someone his own size.

"He was wearing a Clippers shirt, so I said, 'You know, the real reason you're so pissed off is because you're a Clippers fan, and they suck.' He didn't know quite what to make of that. He said, 'Are you a Lakers fan?'

"I said, 'Not really. But if you're going to pick a loser, why not shoot the moon and go with Golden State?'"

When Susan asked him to explain, Will said, "The Warriors lost sixty-five games this year. They finished dead last in the NBA. Anyway, he thought that was funny, and he started to loosen up."

"And you kept talking to him," Susan said.

"Yeah," Will shrugged. "He started getting friendly. Whenever I see an opportunity to bring someone over to my side, I take it. Maybe I'll never see him again, but I know there's one more person in the world who bears me goodwill."

Susan interpreted this statement in the best possible light, as a sign of Will's desire to spread friendship and make peace. Looking back now, after many years of marriage, she was able to interpret the words more accurately. "An opportunity to bring someone over to my side" said a lot about Will, the opportunist who divided the world into his side and the other side.

At the end of the evening of their first date, on the sidewalk in front of her apartment, she stepped forward and kissed him on the cheek. When she stepped back, he looked disappointed.

Oh, I didn't do that right, she thought. *He wanted a real kiss.* She looked down at the pavement, and then back up at him, thinking, *Please don't give up on me. It takes me a long time to warm up to someone. But I'm worth it. I swear I am.*

Watching her eyes as these thoughts passed through her, Will thought she looked like a stray dog in search of a home. "Can I see you again?" he asked.

Her whole face blossomed into the magical smile he had seen that day in the restaurant two years earlier.

"Yes."

The first time they slept together, his passion was clear, and the experience she had feared might be awkward was deeply moving instead. It shook her out of her depression and re-awakened her to life.

That was thirteen years ago. They married within nine months, and for a while she travelled with him everywhere as his business grew. Throughout those early years, his devotion to her was unwavering. She could see in his eyes and feel in his touch that no woman was as beautiful or as interesting to him as she was. At the parties and fundraisers they attended, he made sure she had everything she wanted. When she was stuck in conversation with some bore, he moved in to relieve her. He could see before anyone else when the introvert began to tire under the strain of socializing, and he took her home.

She enjoyed watching him interact with other men. He had an instinctive sense of people's spatial boundaries. He knew exactly where the line was between friendly and uncomfortable. In business interactions, he would slowly maneuver himself into position just an inch inside that boundary. Then he would put his hand on the other man's shoulder, gripping it just a little too tightly while he continued to speak cheerfully. The ambiguity of his touch was calculated to make people confused about whether they should feel reassured or threatened. He was at once their friend and capable of hurting them.

Will could tell a great deal about a person from their reaction to this treatment. The trusting, naive and unsuspecting showed insufficient alarm at these minor trespasses. The fearful shrank back almost imperceptibly. The strong pushed back. The ones in whom he inspired passion and trust leaned into him. From these reactions, he could gauge whether a person would be motivated more by threats or by generosity, whether he should appeal to their loyalty or their self-interest, and how far he might be able to push them.

Each of these interactions was, in its own way, a reenactment of that first scene Susan had witnessed in front of the coffee shop—Will was slowly and subtly taking control of the situation. And though he was tall, physically strong and imposing, he ruled by confidence and charm instead of force. His employees respected and admired him, and Susan admired him too.

So long as the food and sex were good, he was an easy man to please. The predictable rhythms of his appetites, along with his confidence, money, and easy manner, gradually transformed her perception of the world from a place of terrifying uncertainty to one of safety and stability. As the foundation of their marriage solidified, her confidence returned.

With friends and acquaintances, she spoke more freely. Her once placid and unexpressive face began to show more clearly the warmth of her character and the liveliness of her mind.

By the sixth year of their marriage, she was outgrowing her husband. She had tired of the ports of Asia, and of playing the wife of the wealthy importer to an audience of businessmen who appreciated her in broken English. She travelled with him less and less, and spent more time at home in Los Angeles, raising money for the arts and charities with the wives of other wealthy men.

After nine years, she stopped travelling with him entirely, except for vacations. She convinced him to buy a house in Santa Barbara, where she could have a quieter life, in fresher air, away from the traffic and the egos of the city. Will's business was running smoothly then, with the day-to-day operations in the hands of a few trusted managers.

Susan expected him to work less after the move. Instead, he travelled more, scheduling six days away to conduct three days of business. And something in him changed in the past two years. She had a sense of what it was, but she didn't want to admit it to herself until just recently, when news from the doctor forced her to confront what she had been avoiding.

She looked again at the wedding photo with sorrow and regret. *If only I had been a year older when I met you,* she thought. *If only I had been year wiser. A year further removed from that awful time. I might have known better.*

The phone rang as she put the photo back on the dresser.

"Hello?"

"Susan?"

"Hi Leila," Susan said as she walked into the closet and began to browse through the hanging dresses.

"Are you coming to book group tomorrow?"

"No," said Susan. "I don't even know what book you're reading."

"*Victory,*" said Leila, "by Joseph Conrad."

"That's not really a book group book."

"You've read it?"

"A long time ago."

"It's so slow. Is it even worth finishing?"

"Of course," said Susan. "All of his books are. You have to be patient with Conrad, but if you're willing to slow down, he rewards you."

"Well I'm choosing next month's book," Leila said. "*The Echo Maker*, by Richard Powers."

"Ugh. That's an awful book." Susan walked into the bathroom and stood in front of the mirror, examining with disapproval the flesh that bulged around her bra straps.

"He won a prize for that!" Leila protested.

"He should have been punished."

"I hear an echo. Are you in the bathroom?"

"Yes, just looking in the mirror."

"Well I hope you're dressed," Leila said.

"Not really."

"Oh, Susan, don't stand in front of the mirror without clothes. No good can come of that."

"I didn't used to be so... soft."

"You didn't used to be forty. Seriously, Susan, don't stand there looking at yourself."

"Don't tell me you don't do the same thing," Susan said.

"I hung a curtain over my mirror."

"Really?"

"No," said Leila, "but I should. Every time I get out of the shower, I catch a glimpse of myself and think, 'Put some clothes on, you cow. You can't walk around my house like that.' Of course, I've had four kids, so I'm a bit worse for wear. How's Will?"

Susan took a deep breath.

"Oh," said Leila. "Bad subject?"

"Bad subject," Susan said. "I don't know how Will is. He's probably fine." She leaned toward the mirror and examined the little wrinkles at the corners of her eyes.

"Are you two going through a rough patch?"

"I guess you could call it that," Susan sighed.

"Eddie and I have been through some tough times, but they pass. You can get past this."

"I don't know anymore," Susan said.

"Have you considered counseling?"

"There's no point," Susan said. "He's seeing someone else."

"Oh. Oh... I didn't know that. I'm sorry, Susan. I'm so sorry. Are you sure?"

"I'm sure," Susan said.

"Oh, that's terrible. How long have you known about this?"

"I don't know. In my heart? At least a year."

"Oh, Susan. I never would have guessed. That has to weigh on you, but you never show it."

"If I seem composed," Susan said, "it's because I work really hard at it."

"Is there anything I can do to help?"

"No, Leila. But thank you. I have an appointment this morning."

"With who?"

"Someone who will help me out of this mess."

"Well I hope it does you some good. Call me if you want to talk. I miss you. We should talk more often."

"I know," Susan said. "I'm out of touch with everyone these days."

"Well don't be. Call me."

"I will. Bye, Leila."

Susan walked to the closet and chose a simple black dress that suppressed her curves. She brushed her hair until every strand was in line, then filed one polished, manicured fingernail. The others passed inspection.

In the kitchen, she placed several items into a large envelope: two photos of her husband, a photo of his silver Mercedes that showed the license plate, a page printed from Google maps that pinpointed his office, and some papers with his name and age and a description of his furniture business.

Her composure was slipping, but her resolve was not. As she walked to the front door, the tapping of her heels on the stone floor echoed through the empty house, and she refused to release the tears from her reddening eyes.

Chapter 4

"Come on, buddy. Today's the day."

Mark Ready opened his bleary, red-rimmed eyes to see his boss, Gary, standing above him in the small cabin of the boat. Above deck, the halyards clanged against the mast in the gentle waves of the marina.

"What day is it?" Ready asked.

"The day you say goodbye to this boat," Gary said. "Come on. I told you, you had to be out today. Go back up to the house. Is your hangover bad?"

"Just the usual," said Ready, sitting up slowly.

"I have a couple of bags to bring down from the car. Rebecca will be here in a minute. Have you two met?"

"No."

"Well put some clothes on."

Gary climbed out of the cabin, and Ready heard him say something to Rebecca out on the dock. A minute later, Rebecca entered the cabin, where Ready sat on the edge of the berth in his underwear.

"Oh," she said, "I didn't know anyone was down here. Are you Mark?"

"Yes," Ready said.

"Gary told me about you, but I always imagined the guy who took care of the boat was..." She looked him up and down. "... older."

Ready was, in fact, twenty-seven years old and six feet tall. The features of his face were sculpted in perfect symmetry, and his eyes were almost as dark as his nearly black hair.

"I was about to get dressed," Ready said.

"So you watch the house when Gary's out sailing?" Rebecca asked, showing no sign she intended to go on deck.

"Yeah." Ready rubbed his eyes while Rebecca looked around the cabin. "Have you been on the boat before?"

"Twice. But I never saw you before."

"Yeah, I know. Um, I was about to get dressed," he said again in a tone suggesting he would like some privacy.

"Go ahead," Rebecca said.

Ready stood up and she watched him pull on his pants.

"Do you mind?" Ready said. "You're kind of staring at me."

"Sorry. I just didn't realize Gary's sailboat guy... looked like... you."

Ready put his shirt on and grabbed his shoes and bag, then climbed out of the cabin just in time to see Gary, bags in hand, step from the dock onto the boat.

"Did you meet Rebecca?" he asked.

"Yeah, we met."

"What do you think?"

"I don't like her."

Gary laughed. "You have the keys to the house?"

"Yes."

"I'll be back in four weeks. Maybe more, maybe less. We'll see how things go."

"All right," Ready said, shaking his hand. "Have fun out there."

"I left some beer in the fridge for you."

"Thanks," Ready said. He made his way along the dock toward the parking lot.

Gary descended into the cabin with the bags.

"Did he say he didn't like me?" Rebecca asked.

"Were you staring at him?" asked Gary.

"A little."

"He thinks you're attractive," Gary said. He tossed one bag toward the berth at the front of the cabin and dropped the other on the bench by his side.

"I heard him say he didn't like me."

"He gets a lot of attention from the ladies."

"So I'd imagine," Rebecca said. "He's very..."

"Handsome?"

"A little more than handsome," Rebecca said.

"He doesn't like being looked at," Gary said as he unzipped the bag on the bench. "It makes him nervous. He once told me that the worst thing is when an attractive woman stares at him when she's with her boyfriend or her husband. It fills him with conflicting feelings." Gary laughed. "So you were looking at him?"

Rebecca nodded her head with some embarrassment.

"Well, you don't have to be shy about it. People look at attractive people. No shame in that. Hollywood built a whole industry around it."

"How long has he been working for you?" Rebecca asked.

"A couple of years."

"What else does he do?"

"Drinks beer. Smokes pot."

"He doesn't have any other job?"

"Nope. Dropped out of college. The guy has no ambition, but he's trustworthy, and he'd do anything to help a friend."

"Is he a little..." Rebecca pointed to her head. "Slow?"

"No," said Gary. "He comes off that way when he's drunk and when he's hung over."

"How often is he drunk or hung over?"

"Most of the time. To tell you the truth, I think he's a little lost."

"I thought that just looking at him," Rebecca said. "Half of me wants to mother him."

"And the other half?" Gary asked with a laugh as he pulled some shirts from the bag. "What does the other half of you want to do with him?"

Seeing Rebecca's embarrassment, he added, "Oh, come on. What do you think goes through a man's mind? Are women really so different?"

"Aha." He pulled a jacket from the bag and tossed it to Rebecca. "The breeze will be cold once we leave the marina."

On Shoreline Drive, Ready's little blue Toyota made its way up the road toward the heart of Santa Barbara.

Chapter 5

Warren Lane stood at the entrance to the restaurant scanning the breakfast crowd. Trim and upright in his finely tailored Italian suit, his body composed a single straight line. His shirt was custom made and neatly pressed. The old-fashioned cuffs were held together by a set of platinum cuff links. His skin was smooth and deeply tanned from the Southern California sun, and his long nose turned down at the tip. His close-set green eyes were watchful. These features, combined with the thinning hair he combed straight back from his forehead, gave him the appearance of an eagle.

He spotted his prey across the room: Benjamin Schwartz, a tired-looking man sitting alone and staring into the distance. His brown suit hung from his slouching frame like the slack riggings of a neglected ship. Lane walked directly to his table, his pace easy but purposeful. At Lane's appearance, Schwartz snapped out of his reverie.

"Mister Lane?" Schwartz said, standing and offering his hand. "I hope the drive from Santa Barbara wasn't too bad."

Ignoring the outstretched hand, Lane dropped an envelope onto the table and sat in the chair next to Schwartz's.

"Take a look at that," he said.

Schwartz sat down and withdrew the contents of the envelope—photos of him in his business suit, standing next to men he didn't care to remember. He scanned the photos and the stack of printed emails and bank statements for only a few seconds before raising his weary eyes to Lane.

"What do you want?" Schwartz asked.

"You put that deal together, didn't you, Mr. Schwartz? After all those years of honest work, why would you associate with people like that? Hmm?" Lane smiled. "Were you in some kind of trouble? Or did you just need some quick cash?"

"I needed the cash," Schwartz sighed. "I wouldn't have done it if I didn't have to."

"Money laundering is a very serious offense."

"What do you want from me?" Schwartz asked again.

"Fifty thousand dollars."

Schwartz shook his head woefully. "I haven't got it."

"Bullshit. You've got three hundred thousand in your retirement account."

Schwartz shook his head. "No," he said. "I have nothing in there now. My wife's been ill."

"Boo-hoo," Lane mocked.

"Do you have any idea how much insurance *doesn't* cover when a person has cancer? We've drained all our accounts. And my wife..." Schwartz choked up. "My wife!"

Provoked by Schwartz's weakness, Lane said coldly, "Sounds like you bought the wrong insurance. Or married the wrong woman." Then he added with contempt, "You're throwing your money into a sinking ship."

Shocked, Schwartz stared angrily at Lane. "Why were you even investigating me?" Schwartz asked. "I've been above board my whole life. At least, until that." He gestured toward the envelope.

"I wasn't investigating you," Lane said. "I was investigating him." He pointed to one of the men in the photo. "His wife hired me to find out who he's fucking. I just happened to come across you in the course of my investigation."

Lane leaned back with a little smile. "It's one of the benefits in my line of work. You start turning over rocks, you start discovering a lot of things."

"So you extort people?" asked Schwartz.

"I'm not in this business for humanitarian reasons," Lane said.

"But why pick on me? Why not go after him," Schwartz asked, pointing at one of the other men in the photo. "He's loaded."

"Yeah, so's his gun," Lane replied. "There are some people you just don't fuck with. And then there are weaklings like you. You'd never do anything to put your precious family at risk."

Schwartz breathed a heavy sigh. "The best I can do is ten thousand dollars. And you give me all of this stuff. The electronic copies, everything. I want it all destroyed."

"You fucking Jews are always haggling," Lane said with contempt. "I didn't come here to negotiate. I came here to tell you it'll cost fifty thousand dollars to make your problem go away."

"I have no cash right now. None. My son's bar mitzvah is next month, and I have to take out a loan to pay for it."

Schwartz's eyes showed a glimmer of pride at the mention of his son. Lane, eager to snuff it out, said as he picked up the envelope and stood to leave, "Why don't you get him baptized? It's free."

Lane dropped his business card on the table and glided toward the exit. Checking his phone as he walked, he saw an appointment in Santa Barbara. "Shit! I forgot about that."

Chapter 6

At nine that morning, twenty minutes after leaving her house, Susan Moore stood inside a coffee shop stirring cream into her coffee with a wooden stick as she looked over the tables in search of the man she was to meet.

Her eyes returned several times to the bleary-eyed man in the far corner who stared toward the window as if lost in a daydream.

"He's all alone," said the barista behind the counter.

Susan turned to her. "Excuse me?"

"The guy in the corner. You keep looking at him."

"I'm supposed to meet someone, but I don't know if that's him."

"Well, lucky you if it is. He's been sitting by himself for twenty minutes."

Susan crossed the shop and said tentatively, "Warren?"

Startled, Mark Ready stood up and offered his hand. She shook it politely. Without introducing herself, she studied his dark hair and eyes, the symmetry and well-formed features of his face. Her eyes wandered down to his shoulders and chest and then slowly back to his face. He was younger than she expected. The resentment she felt at her unwanted attraction to him showed in her eyes, and Ready interpreted it as a negative judgment of himself. The scrutiny of her sharp, penetrating eyes and the quick mind behind them unnerved him. Seeing his discomfort, she said, "I'm sorry. My name is Susan. Susan Moore."

Ready looked confused and slightly intimidated. *He's hung over*, she thought, and then she asked, "You *are* Warren Lane, aren't you?" She handed him a card that said *Warren Lane, Private Investigator*. Neatly printed in black ink beneath the name it said: *June 21, 9:15 a.m.*

"Um, yeah," Ready replied as he examined the card. "You um...." He looked up from the card to find her still studying his face. He nervously looked her up and down and finished his sentence with, "...that's a nice skirt."

He can't be that stupid, she thought. But what came out of her mouth was, "This is a dress."

"Yeah. Right," said Ready, smiling.

She had already formed her opinion of him: good looking, malleable, not too bright. A screen upon which a younger woman might project her fantasies.

"I thought you'd be a little older," Susan said. To herself, she thought, *I'd have more confidence in a man of forty who wasn't hung over.*

"I might be older than I look," said Ready.

"I doubt it," Susan replied. Her words had a sharp, unfriendly edge. The filter between what she felt and what she said was dissolving. She could feel the layers of the pearl being stripped away, exposing the raw emotion at its center. "Can we get started?"

"Sure. Have a seat," Ready said, pulling a chair from the table.

Susan sat down and hesitated for a few seconds. Finally she said, "I think my husband is having an affair."

"OK." Ready's mind, slowed by the hangover, was just now beginning to assemble the pieces of what was happening.

Susan pushed an envelope across the table to him. "There are some photos of him in here, his work address, a photo of his car, and some other information to get you started. My number's in there too."

"OK," Ready said.

"I want you to find out who he's sleeping with. Get a photo of her if you can. I want to know where they meet and what they do." She stopped and looked toward the window, and her sharp, observant eyes softened in response to her thoughts. Part of her still wanted to admire her husband, the man who had helped her out of her abyss and showed her the way to confidence. His fall from grace wounded her almost as much as his betrayal.

Ready could see the emotions play out across her face. They ended with a look of doubt and weakness, and for a moment he thought she was going to change her mind and call it all off. But she took a sudden deep breath and said in a faltering voice, "He's all I've got, but I can't have him anymore. I just can't."

Ready was caught off guard by the unexpected vulnerability of the woman whose presence so far had only intimidated him. Before he knew what he was saying, his innate kindness propelled a promise from his lips. "I'll do whatever you want," he said. "I'll get you what you need."

"Thank you," she said. She stood and slid a check onto the table, made out to Warren Lane in the amount of ten thousand dollars.

Ready looked at the check then back at her. "There's your retainer," she said. "I'm sorry to run, but…" Her eyes were reddening, and she turned and walked away, saying, "I'll be in touch."

Ready put the check and Warren Lane's business card into the envelope. As he exited the coffee shop a few minutes later, he bumped into a tan, smooth-skinned man wearing an Italian suit. A few drops of Ready's coffee splashed onto the suit. Warren Lane, scowling at the stain, said, "Watch where you walk, you stupid fuck."

Chapter 7

The following morning, Ready awoke at 11:00 a.m., pleased to find himself alone in the guest room at Gary's house, and relieved that his hangover was milder than usual. After toast and coffee and eggs, he picked up his phone and his keys, took the cash from the coffee can under the bed, and drove downtown toward Will's office.

What the hell am I going to do when I get there? Ready wondered. *Stare in his office window? Look through his garbage can?*

He neared the building just in time to see Will's silver Mercedes approaching in the lane of oncoming traffic. He swung his little Toyota around and followed.

The two vehicles proceeded south down the Pacific Coast Highway to Oxnard. Ready followed Will's Mercedes off the highway to a strip mall with a check-cashing store, a Laundromat, and a Mexican take-out. Will drove around the buildings and parked in back where Ready watched him knock on a white metal door.

He looked at Will's expensive grey suit and the knuckles of his big meaty fist and thought, *He's a pretty big guy.*

"Will Moore," said Will in response to someone inside the building. The door opened and Will went in.

A few minutes later, he came back out, examining what looked like a new passport. He slid the passport into the inside pocket of his suit, and then got in his car and drove away.

Ready approached the building and tried to look through window to the right of the door, but it was covered by cardboard on the inside. He went around front to the Mexican take-out and ordered a burrito. For the next hour, he sat in his car.

Finally, he went back and knocked at the door. A man inside asked, "Who's there?"

"Warren Lane," said Ready.

"Don't know you."

"Will Moore sent me."

"Will Moore?" A thin man in his fifties opened the door a few inches. A pair of glasses was perched on the end of his nose, with a thin chain that went around the back of his neck. "What do you want?"

"I need some ID," Ready said. The man opened the door, and as Ready stepped in, he had no idea what to do next. He thought about asking why Will would be getting a fake passport, and where he might be going with it, but how would this man know? Wouldn't he become suspicious if Ready started asking questions about Will after he had just said that Will sent him? He pulled Warren Lane's business card from his pocket, as if looking at it might give him some idea of what a real detective would do next. Susan's check came out with the card.

"What kind of ID you need?" the man asked.

"I just need to cash a check," Ready said.

"License?" said the man. "Stand over there." He pointed toward the camera and the screen in the corner.

Ready stood against the white screen and the man snapped his photo. "Look OK?" the man asked, turning the computer screen so Ready could see it.

"Yeah, that's fine," Ready said.

"What name you want on that?"

Ready handed him the business card and said, "Warren Lane. Use the address on the card."

The man read the card and said, "You're a private detective?"

"I'm pretending to be one," Ready said.

The man typed the information from the card into the computer and returned the card to Ready. "Date of birth?" he asked.

"June 27, 1987"

The man entered the information and Ready heard the whirr of a printer starting up. "It's going to take a minute to laminate," the man said. "That's a hundred and fifty."

Ready counted the curled bills from his pocket.

Two hours later, he was back in Santa Barbara, standing at the counter of the bank that issued Susan's check. He presented the new license and asked to cash it.

The teller looked at the check and said, "I'm sorry, sir, I'm going to have to talk to my manager." After searching in vain for her manager, she had a brief conversation with another teller, who handed her a piece of paper. She brought the paper to Ready and said, "Because of the amount of the check, and the fact that you'll be taking it in cash, we're required by law to fill out this form."

"No problem," Ready said.

The paperwork was soon completed, and Ready left the bank with a stack of hundred dollar bills.

On his way home, he picked up two pre-paid Visa cards and a six-pack.

Chapter 8

As Ready was driving home, Warren Lane sat at an outdoor cafe staring at his phone. His assistant, Maxine, sat across from him watching a waiter and waitress clear plates from a table.

"Did you notice that, Warren?"

"Notice what?" Lane asked.

"The waiter and the waitress. Did you see the way she touched him as she passed? Do you think they're lovers? Or do you think she just wants to be his lover?"

"Why would I care?" Lane asked, not looking up from his phone.

"I was just wondering if it was the type of thing you noticed."

"Not unless I'm getting paid."

"Do you ever look at women, Warren?"

"Not really."

"Men?"

"No."

She nodded. "You have that look about you."

"What look?"

"Asexual. I sometimes think you couldn't find anyone more attractive than yourself."

"Love," said Lane as he put his phone into his pocket, "is just a lever for other people to manipulate you. And sex is just a trick nature plays on the young to propagate the race."

"You're the most cynical man I've ever met."

"That's why I'm good at what I do. There's something dishonest beneath every honest appearance, and I have the instinct to dig it up."

"I would hate to see the world like that," Maxine said. "Do you know why I keep working for you?"

"Because I pay you a lot."

"Yes, and that's the only reason."

"I know. Do you know why I pay you so much?"

"Because I'm worth it."

"Because that's my lever on you. You could do this job for any private investigator in town, but none of them would pay you enough to keep you in that fancy apartment."

"But I *am* worth it. You wouldn't pay me so much if you didn't think I was worth it."

"True."

"I just wanted to hear you say that."

"And now you have," said Lane. "What did you learn about our friend Benitez?"

She shook her head. "Don't fuck with him."

"No?"

"No. I sent you a zip file with some documents and photos."

"All right."

"Just stick to the original investigation. Dunleavy does plenty to keep you busy. Don't go looking for trouble."

"Anything else?"

"Susan Moore called."

"Susan Moore?" Lane said irritably. "She stood me up yesterday."

"Do you want the message?"

"No. And if she calls back, tell her to fuck off."

The waitress left the check on the table. Lane examined it and smiled, then handed it to Maxine. "What do you see here?" Lane asked.

Maxine studied the check and said, "She got the drinks wrong. We both had iced tea, not lemonade. But I think they're the same price."

"Did you notice the table next to us?"

"The guys in suits?"

"Yeah," said Lane. "They had lemonade. And they both had the special, just like us. Do you see what she's doing?"

"The waitress? No."

"She's rolling checks. She prints a check for them and they pay it. Then she gives the same check to us, and she pockets the cash. The system never even knows we were here. As far as the system knows, one table was served and one check was printed and paid. Everything's square."

"How do you know these things?"

"I waited tables in high school. It was a lot easier to roll checks back then, before everyone started using POS systems. Of course, it only works if I pay cash." He slipped three twenties into the leather check holder.

"You're going to make it easy for her?"

"Why not?" Lane asked. "A girl has to make a living."

Seeing the bills protruding from the edge of the check holder, the waitress collected the cash and said thank you.

"Thank *you*," said Warren Lane with a smile.

Chapter 9

That evening, flush with cash, Ready wandered into a sports bar and found the last empty seat at the bar.

"Anyone sitting here?" Ready asked the young Mexican-American man sitting at the next stool. He wore a short-sleeve, collared blue shirt with his name embossed on the front. *Omar.*

The man tore his eyes from the boxing match on TV. "No, you can sit there," he said.

Ready took a seat and ordered a shot of bourbon and a beer.

"I used to spar with that guy up there," said Omar. "I fought so many rounds with him, we're like brothers."

Ready looked at the boxers on the screen. "You mean the white guy?"

"That ain't no white guy. That's Marco. He's Mexican. And the other guy's black. Only white guy up there is the ref."

Ready watched the boxers for a moment then said, "I don't like violence."

"See how the black dude keeps dancin' around? That's the kind of shit that pisses Marco off."

Ready looked at the names stitched into the boxers' trunks. Ramirez was the Mexican. The black fighter was named Thomas.

Thomas landed a hard punch to Ramirez's right side, just below the ribs. Ramirez winced and took a step back. Pursuing him to the ropes, Thomas threw several quick punches to Ramirez's head, none of which landed cleanly, followed by another hard left hook to the body. Ramirez's legs buckled momentarily, but he kept his feet and slipped away from the ropes. He spent the last ten seconds of the round circling the ring to avoid his opponent.

"Looks like your friend is doing the dancing now," Ready said.

"Yeah, he's hurt," said Omar.

The bell rang, and Omar watched the replay of the two body shots. "Marco's gonna knock that dude out," he said.

"How do you know?" Ready asked.

"That guy drops his right when he throws the left hook to the body. He's supposed to keep it up by his chin. Marco sees that. He's gonna knock him out."

When the next round began, Ramirez jabbed and circled to his left.

"See how that dude's head pops back when he gets hit with the jab?" Omar said. "Marco's got a lot of snap on his jab. Used to put big welts on my face. Used to make my girlfriend upset when I'd come home with my face all swollen. Now, look." Omar pointed to the screen. "He's backing up on purpose, tryin' to draw him in. He wants that guy to throw the hook again, so he can time him when he drops the right hand. And there he goes!"

Just as Thomas launched his left hook to Ramirez's body, Ramirez threw a left that connected with Thomas' chin and dropped him to his hands and knees.

"He ain't gonna make the count," Omar said, shaking his head.

Thomas was up at eight, but his legs were wobbly and his eyes were glazed. The referee waved him off. The fight was over.

"Good fight." Omar clapped. "Hey, what's your name, man?"

"Um..."

Omar laughed. "You don't know?"

"Warren," said Ready.

"Nice to meet you. My name is Omar." He pointed to the name embossed on his shirt.

"You a mechanic?" Ready asked.

"I fix elevators. How 'bout you?"

"I housesit for this rich guy when he's out on his boat," Ready said. "When he's back on land, I live on his boat."

"So you're like his little hotel maid," Omar joked. Ready hadn't thought of it this way before. "You like doing that?"

Ready shrugged. "It gives me plenty of free time."

"That ain't always a good thing," Omar said. "He pay you?"

"Enough for food and gas and beer. Actually," Ready added, "I'm doing some detective work on the side."

"Oh yeah?"

"Yeah. I just sort of fell into it."

"How do you fall into detective work?"

"This woman came up to me in a coffee shop asked me to follow her husband."

"Did you know her?" Omar asked.

"No."

"And you just said OK?"

"Pretty much, yeah."

Omar looked at him thoughtfully, and then said, "Hey man, I don't mean to be rude or nothin', but you don't seem real bright. You just go around sayin' yes to strangers?"

"Yeah."

"Life is gonna fuck you up, man."

Ready shrugged. "A few weeks ago I had a moment of enlightenment. I was out on the boat, and I took some acid, and I had this realization: 'Say yes, and the world will open up before you.'"

Omar stared at him for a moment, and then laughed. "So now you just walk around sayin' yes to everyone?"

"Yeah, man. You wouldn't believe all the things you discover when you start living life like that."

"Oh, I can imagine," Omar said. "And that's how you got mixed up with this woman? That's how you became a private eye?"

"Yeah," Ready replied. "But with her, I don't know. I think I would have said yes anyway. I mean, when I said it, it wasn't even a conscious decision. I just heard the words come out of my mouth."

"So now you got all her problems to deal with."

"I guess so," Ready said.

"Do you know how to carry out an investigation?"

"No," said Ready.

Omar nodded. "I guess you just start following people."

"I guess so," Ready said.

"Well you watch it with the yesses, man. A detective has to be cautious."

"I don't think I have much caution in me right now," Ready said.

"Right. You're the enlightened guy floatin' around on the borrowed boat, sayin' yes to everything. What do you got to lose?"

Ready knew Omar had said the words in jest, but he felt their sting. He'd been adrift for years. During his occasional bouts of sobriety, he'd try to get his bearings, but he found himself always at sea. He invariably returned to drink, and every day began with a pounding headache and seasick dread.

"I'm not an enlightened anything." Ready stared sadly into his beer. "I'm actually kind of a loser."

Ready thought about all the women who stared at him. When he was sober, he avoided them because he knew at some point they'd peek behind the pretty face and find a man without skills, direction, accomplishment, or ambition—a man not worth keeping. And in that moment, he wouldn't be able to pretend anymore that his life was OK.

He remembered the cash in his pocket and asked Omar, "Hey, do you like coke?"

"Cocaine? No. I don't touch no drugs."

"Well I need a little pick-me-up."

"It's about time for me to get goin'," Omar said, rising from his barstool.

"I got the tab," said Ready as he pulled a wad of cash from his pocket.

When Omar saw the stack of hundreds, he said, "Damn. Yeah, you can get this one. And watch what you say yes to. With all that money, you're lookin' for trouble."

Thirty minutes later, Ready was in a messy apartment, purchasing seven grams of cocaine from a trust fund kid named Larry who dressed as if he had just stepped out of an REI catalog.

"If you want a really good time, take some of these." Larry rattled a small bottle of pills. "The good times are right in here."

"What's that?" Ready asked.

"A hundred bucks and they're yours."

"OK," said Ready.

Larry handed him the cocaine and the bottle of pills.

On the way back to the house, Ready picked up some beer and a bottle of bourbon.

Chapter 10

The following morning, Ready dragged himself out of bed at 11:30 and drove downtown. He parked a block from Will's office and waited. The cocaine had kept him up past 6:00 a.m., and his hangover was much worse than usual.

He looked down the street toward Will's office, his eyes drooping almost to sleep every now and then. Will emerged at twelve fifteen and drove off slowly. Ready followed him into the parking lot of a retirement home. He watched Will walk into the building and decided to wait for him to come back out. The sun was hot, Ready's mouth was dry, and his head was pounding. He found a bottle of water behind his seat and took a sip. Then he picked up a bottle of ibuprofen from the floor in front of the passenger seat. He dropped five pills into his hand, tossed them into his mouth, and washed them down.

Wait a minute, he thought. *Since when is ibuprofen blue?*

He opened the bottle and dumped out two more pills. Squinting at the word etched into the front of the pills, he read "Pfizer." *That's Viagra*, he thought. He recognized the bottle as the one Larry had sold him the night before with the cocaine.

"Fuck me!" he said slowly. "I'd give a hundred bucks right now for some real ibuprofen."

After fighting sleep for twenty minutes, Ready watched Will return to his car and drive away. Then Ready went inside.

"Can I help you?" asked the woman at the front desk.

"Do you have any aspirin or ibuprofen?" Ready asked.

"I'm sorry sir, we can only dispense medication to our residents. Are you here to see someone?"

"Uh, Mr. Moore."

"You mean Mrs. Moore?" the woman asked. "Lucille. She's in the group activity room." She pointed down the hall.

With its polished linoleum floor, white paneled ceiling and fluorescent lights, the activity room looked like a middle-school cafeteria. One wall was lined with windows looking out on the parking lot. Another was lined with stackable chairs, and in the middle of the floor were several foldable cafeteria tables with attached benches.

Scattered about the tables were a dozen or so elderly residents. At the far end of the room, a band of musicians, looking almost as old as the residents themselves, stood tuning their instruments.

Ready wandered through the room looking at the inmates.

"You lost?" a man asked.

"I'm looking for Mrs. Moore," Ready replied.

"That's her," the man pointed to a woman sitting by herself at a table a few feet away.

"Did I hear my name?" Lucille Moore asked in a stern cranky voice. She sounded like an elderly drill sergeant. Then looking at Ready, she said, "It's about time you got here. Who are you?"

"Warren Lane," said Ready.

"I don't know you," Lucille barked.

"Are you Will Moore's mother?"

"Yes I am."

"May I ask you some questions?"

"You seem to have already begun. Why don't you take a seat? You don't look so good."

Ready sat on the bench next to Lucille and rubbed his eyes.

"Looks like you're ready to check in here yourself," she said. "How old are you?"

"Twenty-seven," Ready replied.

"A fine age," Lucille said. "When I was twenty-seven, I was still single. That was unusual in those days. My mother was worried.

The fellas who used to chase me were such a bunch of dunces, I couldn't bear the thought of marrying any of them. But I liked the attention."

She leaned in close and whispered, "We girls like to play the field too, you know."

"Ohhhh," Ready moaned. "If only I could puke."

"Got a little hangover, have we?"

"More than a little."

"If I had my flask with me, I'd give you a swig. I hate to see a man suffer. Especially one as handsome as you. Now what did you want to ask me?"

"I was going to ask a few questions about your son."

"Well, I'm not talking," Lucille snapped. "Any man comes around here asking about Will, I assume he's an investigator. What's he up to now? Embezzlement? Adultery? Oh, hell, why not both? It costs a lot of money to keep a wife and a mistress. Have you met his wife? She's a lovely woman. Lovely."

"Does he have a mistress?"

"I told you I'm not talking," she barked. "Nosy little thing, aren't you?"

Lucille stood up as the band began to play. "Won't you dance with me?" she asked. "I never have a partner, and you're such a handsome man."

Ready reluctantly agreed, and they began to dance.

After a moment, Ready felt a tingling in his crotch. As the sensation intensified, he remembered the Viagra and he said half aloud, "Oh, shit!"

"Watch the potty talk, mister," Lucille said sharply. Ready looked at her, and she smiled politely.

"Hey, um, I gotta get going," Ready said.

"Oh, come now," said Lucille. "We've just begun to dance."

She pulled him closer, and when she felt his erection pressed against her hip, her eyes lit up and her smile showed a set of bright white dentures. She draped her arms around his neck and pressed herself against him. "When I was a girl," she said, "we had a special way of dancing when things like this arose."

She moved her hands to his hips and pulled him tightly against her. Then she began to rub her thighs and stomach against his crotch. He tried several times to pull himself away, but each time she pulled him back. He realized that from a distance it must look like he was humping her. When he noticed the other residents staring at them, Ready abandoned his resistance and resigned himself to following her lead.

She spoke loudly into his ear. "Of course, our parents never knew we carried on like this. That was during the war, and we girls wanted to do our part for the country. So when the boys were on leave, we did what we could to boost their morale.

"Now, if I could still move my hips the way I could back then, I'd have you wetting yourself in a minute or two. But I've got arthritis now, so you'll just have to take what you can get."

Ready's mouth and throat were dry with mortification. His heart felt as if it were being squeezed by a mighty fist, and time slowed to a crawl. "How long is this song?" he asked.

"Long enough for us to get to know each other," Lucille said.

As the song ended and the next began, she refused to let him go.

"You have very strong arms," Ready observed.

"Oh, now look at poor Elmer over there," Lucille said. "He's jealous."

As they turned, Ready saw an elderly man sitting alone at a table twenty feet away, arms folded tightly across his chest. His thin frame was lost in light-blue slacks and a checkered shirt that were several sizes too large. If he had ever fit into those clothes, he must have shrunk considerably. His oversized eyeglasses magnified his eyes so that he looked like an owl. His brow was furrowed and his mouth was fixed in a sour frown.

"Elmer's a war hero," Lucille said. "Crimean War, judging by the looks of him. He likes to think he's my boyfriend because I sit in his lap on movie night. He kisses well enough, but his equipment is shot. I couldn't get a rise out of him if I put a bicycle pump up his ass. Now you, on the other hand… You have that youthful vigor. Sends a tingling all through me."

Ready now added to his list of woes the image of Lucille trying to inflate the withered Elmer with a bicycle pump. He let out an involuntary sigh, which caused Lucille to pull him closer and say, "Feels good, doesn't it?"

They danced for one more song. When at last she let him go, Ready glanced up through the windows and saw Will's silver Mercedes returning to the parking lot.

Ready walked Lucille back to the table and took a sip of water to wet his throat so he could speak. "Your son is coming back," Ready said.

"Oh, good," said Lucille. "I sent him out for chocolate. The nutritionists here aren't big on sweets, so you have bring your own."

"I really have to get going," Ready said. Then, not knowing the proper etiquette for parting from an elderly stranger who'd just been dry-humping him, he extended his hand for a handshake and said, "It was nice to meet you, ma'am."

Ignoring his hand, Lucille grabbed his cock, gave it a shake, and said, "You've got a real champ there."

Ready ran out through the far exit just moments before Will walked in.

He sat in the parking lot for ten minutes before Will returned to his car. Ready followed the silver Mercedes to a residential neighborhood in northern Goleta. He parked his Toyota and watched Will walk into an expensive Italian-style villa of light grey stone. Then he fell asleep.

Chapter 11

When Ready awoke an hour later, his headache and his erection throbbed in unison. A little girl of seven or eight stared at him through the passenger window. Her features and expression were unusually serious for a child of her age.

"Are you homeless, mister?" the girl asked.

"No," Ready said. "I'm just trying to sleep off a hangover."

"What's that?"

"It's what you get when you grow up to be a dumb-ass coke-sniffing alcoholic," he said.

"My Daddy used to drink," the girl said. "Mommy made him go away."

"Good for her," Ready said. "Say, do you know who lives in that house?" He pointed to the house Will had walked into.

"Miss Ella," said the girl. "She's very nice."

Ready heard the girl's mother call. "Josie! Get back in here and clear this table."

"I gotta go, mister."

"Nice meeting you," Ready said.

"I hope you stop being a dumb-ass and feel better," said Josie.

Ready got out of his car and walked around the side of the grey stone house. The first floor window was a few feet above the ground, so he stepped onto a little slanted ledge and pulled himself up by the drain spout to get a peek inside.

Will was speaking to someone Ready couldn't see. "You know what I like about you?" Will asked.

"What?" asked a bright clear voice.

"You're like sunshine."

Then she glided into view, graceful and lithe in her white skirt and blouse. With her blonde hair, blue eyes, and clear smooth skin, she struck Ready as a vision of summer and light.

Will pinched her behind, and her face momentarily darkened.

"Don't pinch my ass, Will," she said. "You know I don't like that."

He pinched it again.

"Now you're just being rude," she said, and turned away from him.

With a single motion he pulled her back by the shoulder, spun her around and planted a crude unwanted kiss on her mouth.

She stepped back and wiped away his kiss. "Go to work, Will. Get out of here."

Will pointed at her and said, "This... this, I don't like. You're not pretty when you're angry."

"Then don't make me angry," she said.

"But she *is* pretty, angry or not," said Ready quietly.

A pebble struck the back of his head and he turned to see Josie scowling at him from the yard next door.

"It's not polite to look in people's windows, mister."

"It's not polite to throw rocks at people's heads," Ready replied.

She threw another rock and it hit him in the forehead.

"Cut that out!" Ready said.

Will had left the house and was walking to his car. In a moment, he was gone.

Ready looked back through the window and saw Ella sitting on the couch. Her expression changed slowly from irritation to thoughtfulness. The little girl threw another pebble, and this one hit the glass. Ella glanced up toward the source of the noise, and her eyes fixed on Ready for a moment with a strange expression of recognition and surprise.

Her grace and smile returned as she crossed the living room, opened the window, and asked, "Are you the painter?"

"Yeah," Ready replied. "All this trim needs to be scraped before I can paint it."

"Why don't you come around front?" she said.

She met him at the door, and he was impressed by the expensive furniture and rugs. "Nice place," he said.

"Welcome to my cage," she said. Then looking at his face, she asked, "Are you feeling OK?"

"Too much sun," Ready said.

"Uh huh. That would explain why you're so pale. Why don't you have a seat? I'll get you some lemonade."

She led him into the living room, and he took a seat on the pearl-colored sofa. At the back of the room was a dining table with a single chair, and a side table with liquor bottles and glasses.

"Do you have any bourbon?" he asked.

"I have Scotch," she said.

"Oh, that'll do just fine," Ready said.

She poured a glass of Scotch for him and water for herself then went into the kitchen for some ice. In a moment, she returned and handed him the drink. She sat on the coffee table just opposite him. Their knees were almost touching.

Ready took a sip of his drink, then sat back and spread his arms wide across the back of the couch.

"You have a fight with your husband?" he asked.

"Oh, no," she said. "He's not my husband."

Ready felt queasy, and the pounding in his head increased as another wave of the hangover washed through him. Ella looked him over, trying to figure out why he looked so uncomfortable. When she noticed his erection, she smiled and he blushed deeply.

"Nice to see some color in your face," Ella said. "Did you walk in here with that?"

"With what?" Ready asked, pretending not to know what she was talking about.

"With that big smile in your pants?"

"No," he said.

"Uh-huh. So you got it just now, while you were looking up my skirt?"

"I wasn't looking up your skirt. I can't even see up there."

"How do you know you can't see up there if you didn't look?"

"I... Look, that's not the sort of thing I do, OK?"

Ella lifted the fabric between her knees just slightly, and Ready looked instinctively.

"What color is my underwear?" she asked.

"White."

Thinking back on Will's words, Ready thought, *She is a ray of sunshine.* He was already enchanted.

Then she stared at his crotch.

"Stop staring at it," he pleaded. "You're making it worse."

Ella laughed. "You *are* fun," she exclaimed. "Is it your hobby to go peeping in girls' windows?"

"Do you treat all your houseguests like this?"

"No," said Ella. "You're the first guest I've had." Then looking back at his pants, she asked, "Doesn't it hurt when it's pointing sideways like that?"

"Everything hurts," Ready said. The daylight from the window made his brain ache, and he rubbed his eyes to blot it out.

Ella took a seat next to him on the couch and began to rub his cock. For a moment, she stared at his blushing face with a gentle smile and said nothing, delighted as much by his embarrassment as by his arousal.

"You can't help yourself, can you... um... what's your name?"

"Warren," said Ready.

"Warren," she whispered in a teasing voice. "Am I really so pretty?"

Ready looked at her face and rubbed the rim of his glass. "Yes."

"You wouldn't let a boner like that go to waste, would you?"

"I...What?" Ready asked with apprehension.

She stood up and pulled her underwear down to her knees, then shook her legs and kicked them off. She pushed Ready's shoulders toward the head of the couch, pulled down his pants, and climbed on. After a few slow strokes, she began to pick up speed.

"Not so hard," Ready said. "I'm gonna puke."

She ignored him and kept going. Just as the first beads of sweat were forming on her face, Ready felt a powerful wave of nausea. Her right hand squeezed his shoulder as she came, and her loud, happy cry sent a bolt of pain through his brain.

They were silent for a moment. Then, still a little out of breath, she said, "Oh my God, I was so turned on before we started, I was ready to blow." She sat up and studied the pained expression on his face.

"You didn't come, did you?" she asked.

"I'm not... I'm having a bad morning," he said. "Actually, I'm not even horny. I should probably go now."

She smiled and said, "That's not what your body says." She moved her hips slowly up and down, rocking them back and forth at the bottom of each stroke. Her face flushed, and her damp hair matted against her forehead and neck as she pushed into his chest with both hands to steady herself.

"It usually takes me a little while to warm up," she said, still panting. "But with you, it's like riding the rapids. I could come again."

"Please don't," Ready begged. He looked seasick.

"No, seriously," she said. "I could. In like thirty seconds."

Ready closed his eyes and rubbed his temples.

"Why do you keep rubbing your head?" she asked playfully. "Are you concentrating? Is that how you stay hard for so long without blowing your load?" She looked at him warmly and smiled before a more serious look crossed her face. "Oh, God," she said, "I'm going to come! Oh my God!"

She came again and Ready pushed her away. He ran to the bathroom, shut the door, and threw up twice into the toilet. After he flushed and washed his face and mouth, he felt immensely relieved. The queasiness was gone, and the headache was now bearable.

He walked back to the couch, where the bright blonde sprite sat in her rumpled skirt and blouse, knees together, feet on the floor, toes turned inward, like a careless child. Her face glowed with satisfied passion.

"You're still hard," she observed.

Ready looked down and thought, *What do those commercials say? Seek medical attention for an erection lasting more than four hours?* He didn't know what time it was, or what time he had taken the pills. "Yeah," he said, "I think I need some help getting rid of this."

"Oh, I like a man like you," Ella said as she pulled him back toward the couch.

She stood up and removed her blouse and skirt, and then pushed him against the back of the couch and climbed onto his lap. She closed her eyes and moved slowly up and down, savoring every inch of him.

"You're not really the painter, are you?" she asked, her eyes still closed.

"No," said Ready, with a soft moan. He was finally beginning to enjoy himself.

"I know, because we didn't call one," Ella said. "Who are you?"

"I'm a friend of Will's."

"Oh, God!" Ella exclaimed with unexpected violence. She moved her hips more quickly. "That turns me on even more. Oh!" she panted. "If he knew I was fucking his friend, it would kill him! Are you his *best* friend?"

"Yes," said Ready.

"Yes!" she shouted, and she came again. She lay down flat, her chest pressed against his, and tried to catch her breath.

Her mention of Will reminded Ready why he was there. *Fuck*, he thought, *I'm just supposed get a photo for his wife.*

He reached to the floor and fished his phone from his pants pocket.

"Who are you calling?" Ella asked.

"Will," he replied.

"Oh, I want him to hear me scream."

"Just kidding," Ready said. "I just need to take your picture."

"Why don't you take a video?" she asked, moving slowly up and down. "We can show it to Will."

"OK," Ready said, happy to follow the path of least resistance. He turned on the video camera.

Ella sat up and put her face up to the lens and said in a long, teasing voice, "Hiiiiiiii, Will." She shook out her hair and straightened her back. Her breasts bounced as she moved more vigorously up and down. "How do you like this, Will? How do you like my boobs?"

She slapped Ready hard across the face, and he almost dropped the phone. Before he could say anything, Ella shouted, "How do you like that, you little bitch?" She slapped him again. Then she moaned, "Oh, God!"

She pushed the hair from her eyes, and moved slowly up and down, whispering, "That's it, Will. Alllll the way in. And, oh! Almost out. Alllll the way in. And...almost out.

"Are you having fun, Will?" she asked in a breathless voice. "Because God knows I am." She raised her hand to slap Ready again and then let it fall without striking. She stopped talking and her eyes glazed over. She heaved forward with great deep breaths and came so violently this time that spirit, sense, and energy abandoned her all at once. Her sheer intensity carried Ready with her, and he finally spent himself.

The two of them lay on the couch for a long time in languid contentment, their breathing gradually slowing, deepening and synchronizing. Finally, Ella lifted her head, opened her eyes, and said, "You must think I'm an awful slut."

"Oh, no!" Ready protested. "I think you're a wonderful slut. I mean..." He looked her in the eye and said with child-like sincerity, "I've never had a stranger welcome me into their home with such incredible hospitality!"

She laughed. "I like you."

"I can tell."

And then, feeling him grow again between her legs, she exclaimed, "Again? Really? OK, this time you drive."

And so the new lovers passed a pleasant summer afternoon.

Chapter 12

When he left Ella's house a few hours later, Ready found the slip of paper with Susan's number and gave her a call as he drove back toward Santa Barbara.

"Hello?" Susan said.

"Hello," said Ready.

"Who is this?" she asked abruptly.

"Warren Lane."

"Why haven't you returned my calls?" she snapped.

"What? I... You didn't call me."

"Every time I call your office, your secretary tells me to fuck off."

"Oh. Yeah. Don't call her," Ready said. "She's a bitch."

"Did you learn anything?"

"I sure did."

"I'm at the Canary," Susan said. "Room 302. Can you come straight here?" She sounded nervous.

"Yeah," said Ready. "I'll be there in a little bit."

Twenty minutes later, he stood at the open door of her hotel room and watched her pace. Her eyes were animated and alert, darting from thought to thought, showing flashes of anxiety, calculation, wonder, anger and fear. In the coffee shop, her appraising scrutiny had made him too self-conscious to really look at her. She was pretty, but there was nothing remarkable about her until you gave her your full attention. Then her beauty blossomed slowly, as she revealed in little flashes the richness of an inner life. In the depth and warmth of those lively eyes, Ready saw the woman Will Moore had fallen in love with, and he was filled with admiration.

When Susan finally noticed him there at the door, she was struck by the change in his appearance. Unlike their first meeting, when was hung over and lethargic, he now glowed with brightness and energy.

"Wow," Susan said. "You have this..." She searched for the right word. "...aura about you. How can you glow like that? Are you ovulating?"

Ready shrugged and said, "I guess so."

She studied his face, trying to gauge whether he had understood the joke. She finally decided that he hadn't. She reaffirmed her initial judgment of him as handsome and unintelligent, and he became uncomfortable again under her direct and probing gaze.

"Have you ever thought of modeling?" she asked.

Ready looked embarrassed and shook his head. "No."

"You have the looks for it." Then she added in a slightly acid tone, "And the brains. Come on in." She closed the door behind him.

"Do you really need a lot of brains to be a model?" Ready asked.

Susan turned on him fiercely. "Who is she?" she demanded.

"Who is who?" Ready asked.

"Who is this little girlfriend of his? Who's he fucking?"

Ready's mind drifted back to Ella on the couch. "Oh, she's a wonderful girl," he said. Then, realizing that his words hurt her, he changed his tone. "I'm sorry," he said. "I know this is difficult."

"No," she said, trying to recover from his enthusiastic response. "I want to know who she is." She took a deep breath and added, "I want to see this through."

She paused, and Ready could see in the changing expressions of her face a long string of troubling thoughts. He looked around the room and noticed there was no suitcase, only a bag from a clothing store on the bed.

She asked again, with her chin up this time, as if trying to look strong, "Who is she? Who does he love?" But her voice was breaking, and Ready thought, *Oh, God. What have I gotten myself into?* He opened the mini-fridge and took out a bottle of beer.

"I know he's having an affair," Susan said. "You know how I know?"

"I suppose you have a sense of these things when you've been married to someone long enough," Ready said. He took a sip of his beer.

"No. He gave me herpes. Whoever that bitch is he's fucking has herpes."

"What!" exclaimed Ready in a panic. He instantly felt phantom pains shooting through his crotch.

"While I'm at home making his bed and cooking his food, he's out having sex with some little slut. What is it with men? And what's so special about her? Is she beautiful? Is she sexy? Is she good in bed?"

Ready nodded quietly in assent to all three questions and she gave him a curious look. But she didn't inquire further. Instead, she said angrily, "Do you have my photo? I want to know what she looks like." There was fire in her eyes. "Show me!" she demanded.

Ready put his hand on the phone in his pocket, then hesitated. Showing her the video would be like pouring gasoline onto a fire. His reluctance triggered a fierce reaction. "Show me the goddamn photo!" Susan said. She was shaking.

Ready pulled the phone from his pocket and opened the video player. Susan took several deep, deliberate breaths to calm herself. She was just beginning to relax when Ready handed her the phone and tapped the screen to begin the video.

"Hiiiiiiii, Will," came Ella's voice from the phone. Her face backed away from the camera, and her naked breasts bounced up and down.

"Oh my God," exclaimed Susan, dropping the phone. "What the fuck is that? I asked for a photo, not a porno!"

"Sorry," said Ready, feeling embarrassed and confused. "Sorry. I uh...." He had no idea what to say next. The stress of confrontation with a vulnerable, angry, attractive woman paralyzed his mind with anxiety.

Susan stared down at the phone. It was screen-side down on the carpet, but she could still hear Ella's moans of pleasure, and her cursing and slapping. Ready grew aroused at the sound of it.

Susan picked up the phone and sat on the edge of the bed. She reset the video to the beginning and watched in silence.

"It's funny he lets her get on top," Susan said. "He doesn't like it when I'm on top. He's very controlling." She was quiet for a moment, and then observed, "Her boobs are so firm. Mine are..." She glanced at Ready. "Heavy." He sat next to her on the bed and took her hand, turning the screen so they both could see it.

Ella was moving fast and moaning loudly. "She certainly does enjoy herself," Susan said. Then in a tone of great surprise, "Oh my God, she slapped him! I would never do that."

Susan looked at Ready, watching his eyes watch the woman on the screen. "She's really something, isn't she?" Susan asked, watching for Ready's reaction. But Ready was transfixed by the sight and sounds of Ella and made no response.

Susan looked back at the video and said, "This woman has no restraint."

As Ella approached her final climax, Susan began breathing deeply, almost in unison with her. "This is going to be a big one," Susan said, as she watched Ella's eyes glaze over.

After Ella's final cry of pleasure, Susan was quiet for several seconds. Finally, she turned to Ready and said with disgust, "Well I guess those two have something special." Then she narrowed her eyes and fixed him in a penetrating glare. "Wait a minute," she said. "How did you get this video?"

The question caught Ready off guard and his stomach sank with fear. "It was taken from the perspective of the man she's having sex with," Susan said. "Which means..." She stared at him for a long moment with an expression of wonder and doubt, her mind churning with ideas. "Which means you must have hacked into Will's phone and stolen it."

Ready quietly let out a deep breath.

"How did you do that?" Susan asked. "He never lets it out of his sight. He's got a password lock and encryption. God, is this the kind of crap he keeps on there? Are there other videos? Other women? Oh, I don't even want to know." Her anger was rising again. "At this point, all I want is a divorce, and I want his money. Not because it means anything to me, but because it means so much to him."

She shot up from the bed and paced the floor, saying hotly, "Is he fucking anyone else? I bet he is. I want emails, text messages, everything. I want to see him explain himself in court. In front the lawyers and the judge and his mother. And then he can explain to everyone why he deserves to keep his big house and his fancy cars and all his precious fucking money."

"OK," said Ready uneasily as he rose from the bed. "I'll get what I can."

"You get me everything," she shouted. "I paid you ten thousand dollars. You get me everything!"

"Calm down," Ready begged.

"Fuck you!"

"I'm leaving," Ready said calmly. "I'll call you when I have more information."

As he reached the door, Susan called weakly, "Warren?"

Ready stopped and turned.

"I'm sorry," she said. She walked over to him. "This is a hard time for me. My world is falling apart. I know I can be difficult, but I appreciate your help. I really do." She looked up at him with eyes full of regret.

Before he realized what he was doing, Ready put his arm around her waist, pulled her toward him, and pressed his kiss upon her with great warmth. She received it with surprise instead of passion.

He drew away, and she said nothing as she studied his face and watched him grow increasingly uncomfortable. Ready could discern no particular emotion in her face. She had the blank expression of a child who has just unwrapped a gift and doesn't know what it is.

"I'm sorry," Ready said. "I got carried away. I won't do that again."

"Did you think you'd do it the first time?" Susan asked, her sharp eyes still studying his face.

"No. This isn't supposed to be part of... the relationship."

"It's not," Susan said. "But you meant it. You meant that kiss." She continued to look at him without revealing any feelings of her own. Then finally a light of understanding showed in her eyes and she said, "It's suffering."

"What?"

"It's suffering you respond to."

"Yes," he said, turning toward the door. "I'll, uh... I'll be in touch." Ready left feeling awkward and humiliated.

Chapter 13

At his office desk that afternoon, Will skimmed through a number of emails before lingering on one from Jeremy Chen: *$100k that came in today put in index fund. Assuming $200k to follow? Call & we'll discuss.*

Will leaned back with a troubled expression. He checked the time. 5:00 p.m. It was 8:00 a.m. in Hong Kong. He called Chen's cell phone.

"Hello?" came Chen's voice from the other end.

"Where did that money come from?" Will asked.

"What? Oh. The usual place."

"We didn't have any arrangement."

"I don't know about your arrangements," said Chen. "I just know the money came in."

"Shit!" Will said under his breath.

"Is there a problem?" Chen asked.

"Yeah, there's a problem. Go ahead and park the money in the index fund. I'll call you later."

Will hung up. He put his elbows on the desk and rubbed his eyes.

He opened the desk drawer and examined the new passport. "The whole point of this was to be able to go in and out without them knowing," he muttered. He sighed and threw the passport back into the drawer. "Lee wasn't bluffing. They're running the show without me."

He made another call to China.

"Wei, it's Will."

"Good morning, Will," Wei said. "Or good afternoon, I suppose."

"Did you pack up one of those special shipments?" Will asked.

"No. Lee's guys did. They came in with a create and told us to put it in the container."

"They just showed up?" Will said. "Did they say I OK'd it?"

"No. We just assumed you did. They said they'd have another one in four weeks."

"No," said Will. "They won't. I'll be there in four weeks, and I'll straighten this out."

After hanging up, Will leaned back in his chair and folded his arms. He stared at the ceiling for several minutes before the bank manager called with the next piece of bad news.

"Mr. Moore, I'm calling from Third Union about one of your accounts," she said.

"What about it?" Will asked.

"You're wife wrote a check for ten thousand dollars."

"Doesn't surprise me," Will said. "Wait, Third Union? She's not supposed to be writing checks on that account. That account is for..." Will stopped himself, and then said, "OK. Thanks for letting me know."

The woman continued, "A man came in and cashed the check in person."

"OK." Will didn't understand where she was going with this.

"Because of the amount, and because we were disbursing cash, we were required by law to alert the IRS."

"Shit!" Will exclaimed.

"If I'd been here when the man came in, I would have called you before letting him cash it."

Will let out a breath of frustration. "Who cashed the check?"

"A fellow by the name of Warren Lane."

"OK," said Will. "Thank you for letting me know about this."

As soon as he hung up he Googled Warren Lane.

"Private detective," he mumbled. "My wife hired a private detective."

There was no photo of Lane on his website, but he managed to find one after a few minutes of searching. He spent a moment examining the long nose, the green eyes and the slicked-back hair. "Guy looks like a fucking prick," he said.

Will's mind turned back to his wife. *I told her never to touch that account. And ten thousand dollars! What the fuck? The last thing I need is the fucking the IRS looking into my accounts.*

He didn't question why she would hire a detective in the first place. He knew she suspected his affairs. But she had been willing to live with them for this long, hiding her doubts and fears behind that proud facade. He interpreted her silence as a sign of contentment.

He thought about Lane again. With a little prying, a private investigator could cause a lot of trouble. Will looked again at the eagle-like face in the photo. "Little fucking bastard," he said. "I'm going to pay you a visit."

He entered Lane's office address into his phone and watched as the directions appeared on the map. It was less than a mile away. Will put on his jacket and headed to the elevator.

* * *

Warren Lane was just leaving his office as Will cruised slowly by. Will pulled his car to the curb and watched in his rearview mirror as Lane approached the driver side door of a red Audi.

Will got out and walked toward Lane. He examined the man from head to toe, noting the fine suit, the leather shoes and the cuff links. *Likes money,* Will thought. *He looks like the kind who will sell himself to the highest bidder, and I've got a lot more money than Susan.*

"Warren Lane?" Will asked.

Lane, irritated at the way Will had looked him up and down, shot him a dirty look and said nastily, "Who the fuck are you?"

The rudeness of his tone, his arrogance and vanity, and his ugly eagle face aroused in Will such a violent antipathy that before he could stop himself, he punched Lane straight in the nose and sent him to the pavement.

"What the fuck?" yelled Lane in astonishment. He put his hand to his nose to try to stop the gushing blood.

Will pulled him up by his lapels and slammed him against the side of the car. "Listen," said Will, shaking with anger. "There are some people in this world you do not fuck with." He tapped his fingers against his chest. "I am one of those people."

He slammed Lane against the car again and then let him go. On his way back to his Mercedes, Will brought the heel of his hand straight down on Lane's driver side mirror, detaching it from the car.

"And I am another," Lane said under his breath as he watched Will's car pull away. He noted the license plate number. "You just found yourself a world of trouble, buddy."

He looked down at his lapel and frowned at the blood. He tried to wipe it off, but his bloody hand only spread the stain. "Goddammit," he said.

Chapter 14

The following morning, Ready awoke in his car at 8:00 a.m., half a block from Will and Susan's house. For the next two hours, he sat and watched the door, drifting in and out of sleep. When Will finally left the house, Ready followed him to the airport and watched him drive into one of the overnight lots.

He called Susan and said, "Will's at the airport. Is he going out of town?"

"Yes," Susan said. "He'll be back tomorrow afternoon. I should have told you."

Ready hung up and said aloud, "Looks like I have a day off." He picked up a cup of coffee and a sandwich on his way back into town, and then drove toward Ella's house. He passed several open parking spaces and drifted slowly by the front of the house, peeking inside like a shy high-school boy hoping to catch a glimpse of the girl he has a crush on.

There was Ella, in a navy-blue T-shirt and dark-green sweat pants, looking out the window next to the front door.

Ready parked and stood by the car watching her. Her face lit up when she saw him, and she waved him into the house. At the door, she pulled him in and threw her arms around his neck and kissed him.

"If I had your number, I would have called you," Ella said. "Will's out of town."

"Wanna go sailing?"

"Really? Yes. Should I put on a bathing suit?"

"If you want. The water's a little cold, but the sun is nice."

"I'll be back in a minute." She ran upstairs. Ready went to the liquor tray and poured himself a shot of Scotch.

Ella came downstairs a few minutes later wearing the same T-shirt and sweats. "Is it OK if I wear this?"

"Where's your bathing suit?"

"Under here."

"All right. You ready?"

Ella slipped a bottle of sunscreen into the pocket of her pants and said, "Let's go."

As they walked to Ready's car, Ella slid her arm through his and whispered in his ear. "Warren?"

"Yeah?"

"When we get to the car..."

"Yeah?"

"Open the door for me."

"OK."

"Then wait till I get in. Then close it."

"OK," Ready whispered. "Is that the right way to do it?"

"I laid awake last night thinking about you taking me somewhere. I pictured you opening the door for me. It's probably not your style, but it was a nice daydream."

He opened the car door and she smiled as she got in.

As Ready walked to his side of the car, Ella turned and looked at the empty fast food bags and beer bottles that covered the back seat. She touched the divider between the front seats, then examined the greasy residue on her fingers and smiled.

When Ready got in, she said, "You don't have a girlfriend, do you?"

"How could you tell?"

"She wouldn't put up with this," Ella said, waving her hand toward the garbage in the back seat. "Can I see what's in your glove compartment?"

"Go ahead."

Ella opened the glove box. "A bottle opener, some napkins, and... what are these?"

"French fries, I think."

"Just in case you get stuck on the freeway? How long have these been here?"

"I don't know."

"OK, after we go sailing, we're going to the car wash. They have one of those giant vacuums."

* * *

Half an hour later they were on a little borrowed daysailer, trolling slowly out of the marina under the power of an electric motor.

"I'll put the sail up when we're a little further out," Ready said. "The wind's against us. Hold this." He gave her the tiller. "Just keep it straight." Ready crept forward to the cockpit and returned with two bottles of beer.

He offered one to Ella. "No thanks," Ella said. "Too early for me."

"It's already open," Ready said.

"Why don't you drink them both?" Ella suggested.

"OK. Have you sailed before?" Ready asked as he took a sip from one of the bottles.

"Not since I was a kid," Ella said.

"We're going to head straight out toward the Channel Islands, then turn west."

They set out against the wind, and after ninety minutes, they were several miles from shore. The sun was bright and the air was warm. The sound of the wind and waves rushing by was too loud for conversation. While the rudder and the sail consumed Ready's attention, Ella sat near the front of the boat, looking quietly out to sea.

She felt the boat turn, and gradually, land appeared again on the horizon. Ready let the boom swing out to ninety degrees, and the wind filled the sail. The air became still and the noise of the waves disappeared.

Ella turned to see Ready watching her. "I didn't know you had a reflective side," he said.

"It feels so much hotter without the wind," Ella said, ignoring his comment. She took off her shirt and pants. "Why aren't we moving?"

"Dip you toes in the water," Ready said.

Ella joined him at the back of the boat and dipped her toes in. "I had no idea we were going that fast."

"We're going faster than we were before. You just don't feel it, because we're going with the wind."

Ready took a sip of his beer as Ella turned and brought her legs back into the boat.

"Your skin is really pale," Ready said. "Shouldn't you wear sunscreen?"

"Fair, Warren. My skin is fair. Pale means sickly looking. Fair is light but healthy. I have some," she said, picking up her sweat pants from the deck. "It's the only thing I brought."

She squirted sunscreen onto her hand and began to rub it into her arm as she watched the planes take off from the airport a few miles ahead. Ready felt her withdraw. "What are you looking at?" he asked.

She shook her head and said nothing.

"Can I do that?" Ready asked, referring to the sunscreen. He lowered the sail and released the boom. The wind was audible again as the boat slowed. He took the bottle of lotion from her hand. "I'll do your shoulders."

She turned her back to him and held her hair above her neck. At his touch, she straightened her back and the hair on her neck stood up. "You're like a cat," Ready said, as he rubbed the lotion down her spine. "Wherever I touch, your whole body reacts."

She turned suddenly to face him and the unhappy look on her face surprised him.

"I don't know why I respond to you the way I do." She shook her head and looked as if she were about to cry. "This wasn't supposed to happen. I was going to leave, Warren. I had a ticket back to New York. That was my plane." She pointed at the white plane a mile south of the airport. "United Airlines. Two-thirty to Los Angeles." She wiped a tear from her eye, and Ready's anxiety rose at the thought of her going away.

"Why were you going to leave?"

"I can't stay here with Will. That house makes me crazy. I have to get back to my life."

"Did you tell him you were leaving?"

"No," said Ella.

"You were just going to fly away?"

"Yes," she nodded. The rims of her eyes were red, and Ready could see she was struggling to control her emotions.

"Why didn't you go?"

For a long time, she was afraid to speak. Finally, abandoning her defenses, she looked at him directly and said, "I was waiting for you to come back."

Surprised by her confession, Ready asked, "How long were you going to wait?"

Ella looked as if she didn't understand the question, but after a moment, she said, "Until you came back." She kept her eyes fixed on him, as if awaiting the blow she refused to defend herself against. Ready said nothing.

"Does that scare you?" Ella asked. "Because it terrifies me."

"I don't know," Ready said.

"You don't know?" Ella asked with some annoyance. "You don't know if it scares you? Or you don't want to think about it?"

"I don't know," Ready repeated. He looked around the boat as if searching for an exit. "Don't put your life on hold for me. I'm not all that."

"But maybe you are," Ella said. "I want to find out."

"Here," Ready said, handing her the tiller. "Take this too." He handed her the main sheet to control the boom. "I'm going to raise the sail. You'll have to work to pull the boom in. If you feel the boat leaning too far either way, let the rope out."

"I don't know how to do this, Warren."

"There's nothing to crash into out here. Just let go of the rope if you feel the boat tipping. The wind will straighten everything out." Ready walked to the front of the boat and took two beers from the cockpit.

"Where are you going?" Ella asked.

"Away."

"Don't just leave me here. I was talking to you. Warren!"

Ready sat alone on the bow for the next half hour, facing away from Ella, drinking beer and watching the shore consume more and more of the horizon as it approached. Ella glanced at him every few seconds during her first minutes in control, hoping he'd come back to finish their conversation; but after a while the rudder and the sail consumed all of her attention.

When she drifted off course, she needed tremendous arm strength and leverage to pull the boom in toward the boat. Over time, she learned to correct her course and let the sail out to ninety degrees, where it required less management and gave more speed.

Each time the boat straightened out, she again had the sensation they had stopped moving, and she occasionally dipped her hand into the sea to feel their speed. Each time, she was impressed.

Ready returned to the tiller to guide the boat around the seawall and into the marina. They didn't speak until Ready asked her to tie up to the dock. Her cheeks were red from the sun, and her back and arms ached from the strain of managing the boom. As he stepped onto the dock, Ready stopped in front of her and said, "I'm sorry. I'm doing my best." A hint of her natural brightness returned. She took his hand and they walked together to the car.

Ella drove, and they stopped at the car wash on the way back to Goleta and got rid of all the beer bottles and fast food wrappers in the back seat. When they pulled up in front of the house, Ella smelled like French fries, and Ready smelled like stale beer.

"You want to come in?" Ella asked.

"What if Will comes back?"

"Beat him up."

"He's a pretty big guy," Ready said.

"But you'd give him a good fight if you really loved me, wouldn't you?" she teased.

Ready looked doubtful.

"Oh, I can see the conflict in you." She smiled broadly. "'Am I more horny, or am I more scared?'" She laughed, and then said, "He's not coming back, Warren. He's out of town till tomorrow. You would have remembered that if you hadn't had six beers."

She put her hand on the inside of Ready's thigh and whispered, "You know what we're going to do when we get inside?"

"What?"

"Nothing." She kissed his cheek and smiled and said, "You're not getting anything for the way you treated me out on that boat."

"Wait, are you serious? I can't tell if you're serious."

Ella shrugged. "Why don't you come in and find out?"

She got out of the car and walked toward the house. Ready got out a few seconds later and followed her to the door.

As they entered the house, Ella said, "I have to take a shower, to wash off the sunscreen and your disgusting car. Wanna watch me undress?"

"Right here?" Ready asked. They were standing at the bottom of the stairs.

"Right here."

"OK."

"OK," Ella said. "You go first."

"What?"

"Fair's fair," she said. "You can watch me undress, but you have to get undressed first."

Ready hesitated, and then Ella took off her shirt and stood looking at him in her sweats and bikini top. "Well?"

Ready took off his clothes and Ella smiled. "Look at you, all ready to go! And I'm not even undressed yet. That's flattering, Warren." She tapped his chest and said, "I wish the top half of you was as enthusiastic about me as the bottom half."

Ella took off her sweat pants and bathing suit. "Now you can wait for me while I shower," she said. "And your aching cock will know what my heart felt like when you left me blowing in the wind out on that boat. If you can't hold out, there are some napkins in the kitchen. You can take care of yourself."

Ready looked at her in astonishment. "I can't believe how brazen you are."

"Good use of vocabulary, Warren," Ella said with a smile. "I told you this house makes me crazy." She stepped forward and kissed him. "I won't leave you hanging. I'm not that much of a bitch." Then she whispered, "And I'm as turned on as you are. But I can hide it, and you can't."

She turned and Ready watched her ascend the stairs. She stopped at the top and said, "Go sit on the couch, Warren. I'll call you when I'm out of the shower."

* * *

A little while later, Ready emerged from the bathroom wrapped in a towel. Ella sat on the bed, naked and cross-legged, with her back propped against the pillows. On the sheet that covered her legs was Ready's empty wallet, along with his license, the pre-paid Visa cards, and some cash. Ella was scrolling through his phone.

"Whatcha doin'?" Ready asked.

"Looking through all your stuff."

"Why?" The tone of his voice and his relaxed posture showed he was at ease with this.

"Because it would take me days to get all this information out of you," she said. "OK, you have two hundred sixty-two dollars in cash, a license, and two Visa cards. Prepaid. And that's it. Is your life really that simple?"

"I try to keep it that way."

"Oh, and this." She picked up his new license from the bed, waved it, and said, "You're going to be twenty-eight in a few days. Happy birthday."

"Thanks. How old are you?"

"Twenty-four."

She turned the screen of his phone toward him and said, "You have a lot of women in here."

"I don't even know most of them."

"I thought you said you didn't go looking up girls' skirts."

"I don't," Ready said. "I just get drunk and things happen."

"Why were you so shy with me? It doesn't seem like you were shy with..." She began reading names. "Ashley, Christine, Devon, Frances, Kate, Kate, Kate, or Kate. God, Warren none of these women have last names. How do you know which Kate you're calling?"

"I don't call any of them," he said.

"Really?" she asked with a look that sought reassurance.

"Really."

"Susan texted while you were in the shower."

"What did she say?"

"She asked if you could meet her at the hotel," Ella said with a wounded look in her eyes. "I hope you don't mind, I texted her back."

"What did you write?"

"'Will you be naked?'"

"Oh, shit."

"She texted right back, 'Not appropriate. Call and let me know when we can meet.' Who is Susan?"

"Someone I work with," Ready said.

"Oops. Sorry."

"It's OK."

"Do you mind if I delete all these other women?" Ella asked, holding up the phone.

"Go ahead," Ready said.

"Is there anyone I should save? Your parents?"

"And Susan. And Marie, my sister. And all the male names."

"You're going to have like eight people left in here when I'm done."

"That sounds about right."

"You're not very social, are you?"

Ready shrugged. "I have my moments."

"I'm putting my number in here, so you can call me. You will call me, won't you, Warren?"

"Of course."

She smiled and typed in her number. "You must get drunk a lot," Ella observed as she began deleting names one by one.

"It cures my hangovers," Ready said.

"And causes them. But you weren't drunk with me."

"No."

"Does that mean I'm special?"

Ready thought for a moment and then said, "Yes."

"Well I think you're special too."

"You like the way I look," Ready said.

"I like who you are."

"Who am I?"

"A kind person, with a good heart. Who's a little lost. Like me."

"How do you know that?"

"I just do," Ella said. "I knew it as soon as I saw you."

"Maybe you just thought that," Ready said, fearing that she was spinning fantasies about him that he wouldn't be able to live up to. "Any man would look appealing to a woman in your situation."

Ella's face clouded. "That was mean, Warren."

"I'm sorry," he said.

She saw that he was, and as she studied his face, the wounded anger in her eyes gave way to curiosity. Though Ella's gaze took in as much as Susan's, it did not arouse in him the same discomfort. He turned toward her rather than away, and confessed to her with an open face, "I didn't mean that the way it sounded. I meant… just don't start building up expectations about me. Don't expect to find something that's not there."

"But there is something there, Warren. I know it."

"Well, I hope I don't disappoint you."

Ella shrugged. "Then don't."

Returning her attention to the phone, Ella asked, "How does someone meet two Talulahs?"

"Same woman. Two phone numbers."

"Deleted," Ella said with a smile. "Come here, Warren," she said, patting the bed beside her hip. "Come be with me."

Chapter 15

Two hours later, Ready sat at the table at the rear of the living room, looking at the weather forecast on Ella's laptop. Ella lay on the couch, paging through *Vanity Fair*.

"You make me nervous, sitting over there at the computer," Ella said.

"Why?"

"That's where Will sits when he does his work. With his back to the wall, so I can't look over his shoulder. He even keeps the curtains shut, as if the neighbors might try to read his email and learn all about shipping rates and customs procedures."

Looking back at her magazine, she said, "You know, this thing is just a catalog. They throw in some stories as an excuse to get people to look at all the ads."

"I don't read magazines," Ready said.

"You know, I was almost in here once," Ella said.

"In *Vanity Fair?*"

"Mmm hmm. In an ad, I mean. They did a shoot with two models. Me and this other girl. They chose one of her photos. I don't have the right look."

"What did they do with your photos?"

"I don't know." Ella shrugged. "Threw them away, I guess."

She stood up from the couch and carried the magazine to Ready. "See that girl?" She pointed to an ad. "I used to work with her. She's really sweet."

Ready looked at the woman in the photo. "Damn, she *is* sweet."

"Warren!" She swatted him playfully on the shoulder.

"How'd you wind up with Will?" Ready asked.

"Oh... I was in Miami between shoots and I met him at this big pretentious party. We talked and had drinks. He took me out to dinner and spent five hundred dollars on wine. I'm embarrassed to admit it, but that impressed me.

"He's generous when he wants to be. He listened to me and he thought I was funny. He has this confidence that the little twenty-something boys don't have. And he wasn't forward or pushy. He didn't brag. Though I suppose dropping five hundred dollars on wine is a form of bragging."

"But he's like fifty," Ready said.

Ella looked embarrassed. "He doesn't look that old," she said. Then she added in a more defensive tone, "I thought he was maybe forty."

Ready's remark stung, and she wished her answer wasn't so weak and evasive. Then she said in a sharper tone, "I don't know, Warren. Sometimes I look for trouble, OK? I *want* to do the wrong thing. I wanted to fuck with him because it was dangerous and bad, and then I wanted to fuck him too, OK? And you know what? I enjoyed it. I really did. Does that disgust you?"

Ready said nothing. She searched his face for a hint of judgment but found none. She felt ashamed, but she wanted to tell him everything.

"When I came out here, I started sinking. I missed my shoots in LA. The agency fired me. I kept telling myself I'd fly back East, tomorrow or next week. And I kept not doing it." She looked at Ready's face, searching again for the judgment she both courted and feared.

"And I didn't do it again today. I didn't fly back," she said. She paused a moment, then said, "Warren, I hope you don't think I go around sleeping with everyone I meet. I mean, I know from how we met it might be hard to think otherwise. But that's not who I am."

"I don't really care what you do when I'm not around," Ready said.

"But I want you to care!"

Ready stood up and kissed her. "I think you're wonderful," he said.

"Do you really?"

"I do. And I *do* care what you do when I'm not around. I just don't like to think about it. You live in some other guy's house, and I'm your...pool boy."

"Warren, I can't stay here."

Ready sat down again and looked at the computer. "What are you going to do?"

"I don't know," Ella said. "You want some iced tea?" She walked toward the kitchen.

"Sure," said Ready.

She returned with two glasses. "You've been studying that weather forecast for an awfully long time. Are you going to take me out for a picnic?"

"No. I was just wondering... how do you hack into a computer?"

"You don't have to hack into it," Ella said. "It's open right in front of you."

"No, I mean, if I wanted to hack into someone else's computer."

"Why would you want to do that?"

"Let's just say I wanted to."

"I don't know," said Ella. "Steal their password. Why are we talking about hacking into computers?"

"I want to get some files from Will's laptop. And his phone."

"Why?"

"I have this feeling he's doing something he shouldn't be doing."

"Like keeping a mistress?" Ella asked.

"Or maybe...getting into some business that's over his head."

"Warren, you're a terrible liar. If you want my help, just ask for it."

"Will you help me steal files from Will's computer?"

"Absolutely."

"How can we do it?"

Ella shrugged.

"Well, keep it in the back of your mind. Maybe you'll get some inspiration."

Chapter 16

Will returned from his trip the following afternoon. On the drive home from the airport, as the radio announcer reviewed the stock market numbers, Will decided he would say nothing to Susan about the check. If Susan was having him investigated, it would be to his advantage if she thought he didn't know.

He thought about Warren Lane and wondered what type of information he was after. He wondered how long would it take Lane to discover Ella. And how far would he dig beyond that? Would the investigation extend to his business?

As Will slowed for a red light, a woman on the radio reported that federal investigators and an international pharmaceutical company were looking into reports of counterfeit cancer drugs. Will turned up the volume.

"These drugs are ideal targets for counterfeiting," the woman said. "Unlike many other medications, they don't have an immediate effect, and the patient can't tell right away if the drug is working or not. That makes counterfeits difficult to identify. These medicines are also very expensive. A counterfeiter can make thousands of dollars from just a few doses.

"Federal investigators are taking this very seriously. The drugs bring in billions each year for the manufacturer, which issued a statement today expressing concern for patient safety and assuring that the counterfeits will be removed from circulation."

A local man named Benjamin Schwartz described his wife's struggle with breast cancer and the possibility she may have received counterfeit drugs. "What kind of person would do something like that?" Schwartz asked. "Just for money? How can someone prey on cancer patients? How do I explain to my son that there are people like this in the world?"

"Jesus Christ," Will said with a heavy sigh as he switched the radio off. He walked into the kitchen a few minutes later to find the island set for dinner.

Susan had spent the day running errands she didn't need to run, just to have something to do. In the house she felt trapped, and outside of it she felt unmoored. In the half-dozen shops she wandered through, she couldn't bring herself to buy anything except a bottle of wine and two steaks. It was easier to think about what needed to be done for dinner than to think about what her husband had been doing, or what might come next in her life.

She found comfort in the routine of cooking: putting the steaks on the grill, uncorking the bottle of Cabernet, turning the asparagus in the pan. When Will returned, she wouldn't be alone. He would be pleased with the meat and wine that always pleased him, and she could listen to him talk about his trip instead of having to listen to her own thoughts.

Will put his bag down and looked through the mail as Susan removed the steaks from the grill and set them on the plates with potatoes and asparagus.

"How was your trip?"

Will looked up from the mail with a hint of annoyance.

"Oh, one of those days," Susan said. "A little time, a glass of wine..."

She held up the bottle of Cabernet. Will nodded his approval, and then returned his attention to the mail as she poured a glass for him.

He put the mail aside and picked up his wine glass without looking at her. Something in his manner soured her all at once, and she thought, *Why did I cook for you? Why did I look forward to seeing you? I didn't. I needed distraction and something to do, and now you're here and I hate you.*

She missed the dirty look he gave her as he took his seat and he thought, *Why are you putting on this show? I know you hired a detective.*

They were silent for a moment before Susan said, "I forgot to tell you I talked to Leila the other day. She says hello."

Will turned his shoulder to her and looked at the wall as he ate in silence.

"How's your steak?" Susan asked. She wanted him to like it, and she wanted him to choke on it. "Did I cook it OK?"

Will glanced at her from the corner of his eye and said nothing. He took another bite of steak and fixed his eyes again on the wall.

Susan laid her knife and fork on her plate and her posture deflated as she let out a sigh. *What right do you have to be angry with me?* she wondered. But his coldness hurt, and finally she asked, "What's wrong? What did I do?"

Will thought, *You wrote a check for ten thousand dollars from an account I told you not to touch, and now the bank is filing papers with the IRS. You hired a detective to investigate me. Do you have any idea what you're getting us into? Do you? You fucking idiot!*

But he said nothing. He glanced at her for just a second as these thoughts went through his mind, and the cold, distant anger in his eyes finally made her confess to herself, *You can't avoid this, Susan. You can't go through the motions and pretend this marriage isn't over.*

These thoughts caused an involuntary shudder. Will turned sharply toward her, pointing his knife, and said, "Don't start your fucking crying. I have enough on my mind without that. Go upstairs and cry."

Susan went upstairs, and Will poured himself another glass of wine. A few minutes later, she stood at the entrance to the kitchen with an overnight bag. "I can't stay here, Will. I need some time away. I'll be at the Canary. Call if you need me, OK?"

"OK," Will said. "Take as much time as you need. I'm sorry I yelled at you. I have a lot on my mind right now."

"Bye, Will."

"Bye, Susan."

In the car, her hands shook, and she had trouble getting the key into the ignition. As she left the driveway, she asked herself, *What were you thinking? What did you think would happen when you saw him? Did you think it would make you happy? And you shopped for him? And you cooked for him? What if he wanted to kiss you? What if he wanted to have sex? You know you will never touch that man again. You will never be close to him again.*

She pulled the car to the side of the road and bent forward as if someone had punched her in the stomach. She felt the full weight of the grief she had been avoiding for more than a year. It was a physical feeling, a crushing of her heart and her intestines. The sheer power of it terrified her. Her instinct was to flee, but there was nowhere to go, no way to run from her own heart.

She couldn't say how long she sat there, but it seemed late when she arrived at the hotel, and she fell asleep with her clothes on.

Chapter 17

After Susan left, Will called Ella. "What're you doing?" he asked.

"Just a little housework." Ella was on the couch, sewing a hidden pocket into the top of one of the living room curtains.

"I'm coming over," Will said.

"Oh, Will, not tonight."

"I won't bother you. I have a lot of work to do. And this place is depressing. I'll be there in twenty minutes."

"Can you make it thirty?"

"OK, thirty."

"You're a doll," Ella said as she held the curtain up in front of her for inspection.

"See you soon," Will said.

Ella hung up and slipped her phone into the little pocket she had sewn into the back of the curtain. She felt through the fabric for the smooth lens of the camera, then used an X-acto knife to cut a tiny circle just large enough for the lens to peep through.

She hung the curtains back on the window behind the table and slipped her phone into the pocket just above the rod. The weight of the phone made the top portion lean slightly forward. She turned on the video camera and sat at the table and pretended to type. Then she checked the video.

A few minutes later, Will greeted her with a kiss on the cheek. She could smell the wine on his breath.

"Nice to see you, sunshine. I have to do some work, and I'm not in a good mood."

"OK, Will. I'm going to watch TV upstairs."

"How about watching on the couch? Use the iPad. I like to look up and see you when I work. It soothes my mind."

"OK."

"And put the headphones on. I can't work when the TV is talking."

"Sure."

Will put his computer and phone on the table in front of the curtained window, and then went to the bathroom.

Ella quickly turned on the camera hidden in the curtain, then went to the kitchen and uncorked a bottle of the heaviest red she could find. She returned to the living room just in time to see Will logging in to his computer, the little camera peering over his shoulder.

Ella put the glass on the table.

"Not so close to the computer," he said. He lifted the glass and took a sip, and then set it down a foot away.

For the next hour and a half, Ella lay on the couch watching the iPad while Will worked. She turned periodically to check the wine glass. Will, thinking she was looking at him, returned her look with a smile.

She refilled his glass several times, eventually dipping into a second bottle. As she entered the living room with the fifth glass of wine, she saw Will type his passcode into the phone that lay flat on the table. She looked up at the hidden camera and a little thrill ran through her.

When her eyes returned to Will, he was looking directly at her. "Had a little thought there?" he asked. "Something in you just lit up."

Ella smiled and shrugged.

"Well, I'm afraid it won't be tonight," Will said. His eyes were heavy. "I'm gonna pack it in. Too much red wine always puts me under."

She followed him upstairs and waited in the bathroom while he undressed. She stayed there until she heard him snoring. Then she went back downstairs and retrieved the phone. The battery was dead. She plugged it in and found the video. Then she set her computer and an external hard drive down on the table.

She replayed the section of the video that showed Will typing his password. She zoomed in and followed his fingers again and again until she was able to discern *TheGoodLife*.

With that she logged into his computer, plugged in the external drive, and started copying everything. The little dialog on the screen said "5 hours remaining."

She scanned through the video on her phone, looking for an instance of him typing the passcode into his phone. She found one 10 minutes into the recording. Again she zoomed and replayed and studied the movements of his fingers. 73719. She unlocked his phone, plugged it into her computer, and copied off everything she could. Then she returned the phone to its charger. She leaned back and took a sip from his wine glass, then went upstairs and set the alarm on her phone for 6:30 A.M.

Chapter 18

When Ella awoke the next morning to the gentle chirping of the alarm, Will was still asleep. She used the toilet and had just begun to brush her teeth when she saw Will through the crack in the open door. He was on his way out of the room. Remembering the hard drive she had left plugged into his laptop, she yelled in a panic, "Will? Will!"

Will stopped at the top of the stairs, alarmed by her tone. "What is it, sunshine?"

"There's a rat in here. A big one."

She ran from the bathroom, past Will and down the stairs, calling, "Get him, Will. I hate those things. Get him!"

"Aw, fuck." Will walked back toward the bathroom.

Stepping lightly across the living room toward the computers, Ella yelled, "Get him, or I'm never going back upstairs."

Ella yanked the hard drive cable from his computer and a little message appeared as she folded the laptop shut: "The disk was not ejected properly."

"Shit!"

She put her computer and the external drive into a drawer in the kitchen, and began to fill the coffee maker. In a moment her heart stopped racing and her easy smile returned.

"I don't see any rat up here," Will called from the bathroom. "And I don't hear anything moving. Where did you see him?"

"He ran right across the sink," Ella called back.

"Arrogant little bastard," said Will under his breath.

"Why don't you just call an exterminator, Will? Save yourself the trouble."

"Good idea," Will called back.

He came down a few minutes later, looking irritable. "Red wine gives me a headache," he said. "And rats piss me off."

Ella poured a cup of coffee and handed it to him.

Will went straight to his computer and logged in. He squinted at the screen.

"The disk was not ejected properly? What the fuck is that supposed to mean? I don't want to hear about your fucking problems." He dismissed the message and began to browse through his email.

Seeing he was in a bad mood, Ella took her coffee out to the front step and sat quietly enjoying the summer air.

Chapter 19

In his office later that morning, Warren Lane sat on the corner of Maxine's desk as he looked through a stack of mail. "Did you manage to dig up anything on William Moore?" Lane asked.

"Not much," Maxine said. "He imports furniture and art from Asia. High-end stuff. He also supplies a couple of wholesalers, and he runs showrooms of his own. Santa Barbara, LA, and Palo Alto. He closed his stores in Portland and Seattle last year. I'm not sure why. He occasionally ships things for museums in Santa Barbara and LA. Mostly stuff coming out of Asia. When the art museum sent that whole exhibit to Tokyo a few years ago, he handled all the shipping. He also brought in the stuff for the Chinese art exhibit last year."

"But you don't have any dirt on the guy?"

"He travels a lot, as you'd imagine in his line of work. What he does when he's abroad, I don't know. But there was this one little blurb in the local news last year."

"What's that?" Lane asked.

Maxine handed him a printout of a newspaper article and he read the title aloud. "Rare Artwork Destroyed in Transit." He read silently for a minute, then said, "Now that's odd. Just this one piece broke?"

"Just that one."

"Might be worth looking into," Lane said.

"I also found this," Maxine said, pointing to her computer monitor. "He set up this trust that includes an investment account and a house in Goleta."

"That's worth a look too," Lane said.

An hour later, he drove up to look at the house. He found Josie standing on the front walk, a stick of fat pink chalk in her fist. She watched him warily as he approached, but she didn't back away.

He stopped less than a foot from her and leaned down until his face was so close she could smell the mustard on his breath. Seeing her draw back at the odor, Lane said, "Hhhhhhhhhhullo, little girl," polluting her air for his own amusement. "Do you know who lives in this house?"

"That's none of your business, Mister."

"Do you speak to your father like that?" Lane asked, standing upright again.

"My father's dead," she lied.

"What a shame. Can you tell me who lives here?"

"No!" Josie said defiantly.

"You know I can just go read it off the mail."

"You stay away from Miss Ella's house!"

Seeing that she was beginning to tremble, Lane bent down again and leaned in so close that when he spoke she was looking into his mouth.

"You know what I want you to do?" Lane asked. He lowered his voice to a whisper and said, "I want you to..." Then as loud as he could, he shouted, "Run home!"

Josie dropped the chalk and ran full speed from the yard.

Ella was just opening the door, with her car keys in hand, as Lane was ascending the steps. "What's going on?" she asked. When caught off guard, her voice had a soft, juvenile quality.

Lane looked her up and down and finding nothing to critique, said, "Looks like Will's got himself a little school girl."

He leaned toward the door to get a look inside, but Ella shoved him back. "Get out of here, you fucking creep!" She watched him with disgust as he strolled back to his car and drove away.

When Will arrived at the house half an hour later, Ella was still out. Josie's mother came storming across the lawn in a rage.

"I don't care what you do in that house over there, but I do not want to see that man around here again," she yelled.

"What man?" Will asked.

"The one who was at your door half an hour ago. He screamed at Josie. She ran into the house shaking and crying and she won't come out of her room. She's terrified."

"What man? Who are you talking about?"

She described Warren Lane, and Will began to bristle. "That man is a fucking prick," he said. "If I ever see him again, I'll knock his teeth right down his throat."

Surprised by the violence of his reaction, the woman's anger abated, and she said, "You don't have to go that far. Just keep him away from here."

Will shook his head. "He won't come around here again."

Ella returned fifteen minutes later to find Will's car in front of the house. She left the box of birthday candles on the floor behind the couch and walked into the kitchen. Will sat at the counter with a half-empty cup of coffee, reading email on his phone. His lips were white with frosting from the cake she had made as a surprise for Ready's birthday.

Will turned with a smile and said, "Oh, hey, Sunshine. Did you make this? It's really good."

Ella looked at him angrily.

"What? I said it was good. Learn how to take a compliment. What's the matter with you? Is it that time of month?"

"Yeah, I'm having my period, Will. Why don't you get the fuck out? The playground is closed today."

"What the hell?" he said, as he rose abruptly from his seat. "Lighten up, will you?"

He picked up his keys and phone from the counter and said, "Let me know when you're back in business."

She stood with her hands on her hips, firmly planted in her disappointment as she watched him leave. The clouds lingered upon her face for the rest of the morning, and her spirit remained low.

At noon, Ready called. "Hey babe. Let's go out and get some lunch."

Ella instantly brightened. "OK. Take me someplace cheap."

"Someplace cheap?"

"Well, not cheap. Mid-range. We can't go anywhere expensive. I don't want to run into Will."

"Oh, so Will takes you out to the fancy places? And I'm your ghetto boy?"

"I'd take the ghetto with you over the world with him," Ella said.

Chapter 20

Around noon that same day, Susan arrived at an Italian restaurant to find her lawyer already seated at a table, sipping water and reading the menu.

"Sorry I'm late, Martin."

"It's OK," he said as he stood to greet her. "I started running the meter ten minutes ago."

She looked at him with some uncertainty.

"I'm kidding, Susan."

"Oh. Sorry. I'm a little off these days."

"I can tell. I probably shouldn't be joking with you."

"No, I need a little levity. Just, next time, make it a funny joke."

The waitress stopped by and explained the day's specials while a busser refilled Martin's water glass.

"Would you like a drink to start?" asked the waitress.

"I'll have a glass of Chardonnay," Susan said.

"Drinking at lunch?" Martin asked.

"Why not?"

"I'll have an iced tea."

Susan waited for the waitress to walk away, then turned to Martin and began to unburden herself, "I've known for a long time that this marriage would end in court, but even two weeks ago, I didn't think we'd be sitting here today. It's all happening so fast. Sometimes I wish I was a weaker person. I wouldn't have lasted this long. The marriage would have ended a year ago, and I'd be on to a new life. But I'm stubborn and strong-willed, and I hold on when I should let go."

"You *are* stubborn," said Martin, relaxing back into his chair. "That's a strength and a weakness."

"It's a weakness," she said. "In me, it's a weakness. I knew something was wrong a year ago, but I pretended everything was OK because I was scared of finding what I knew I'd find.

"I'm a coward, Martin. I'll do anything to avoid pain. I'll procrastinate. I'll lie to myself. I'll pretend. Anything to delay the hurt just one more day.

"But I'm done running. I'm done pretending. And now..." She stopped and thought for a moment. "Do you know what kinds of thoughts go through my head now?"

Martin looked at her and waited silently for her to continue.

"I think, 'Are my friends talking about me? Do they talk about what a failure all this was? Do they talk about how Susan, who's so smart and so together, let herself be betrayed?' And what comes next? Where do I go from here?"

She looked at Martin directly and said, "I'm scared of what's next. I can't see it. It's just a void." The look of worry on her face was painful to behold.

"There was a time when I had faith in myself," she said. "A long time ago. Before I knew just how wrong things can go in this world. But now... I don't know.

"I keep looking for that faith, and it isn't there. I have this fear, deep in my heart, that a breakdown is coming, and I'm going to need that faith to pull me through. But it isn't there, Martin. It isn't there. And I don't know quite who I am anymore."

"Well," said Martin, "the hard part is coming. Are you sure you're ready to see this through?"

She took a deep breath and nodded. She didn't look at him; her eyes were focused straight ahead.

"And you have evidence of his affair?"

"You can talk to my doctor about that. I also have a video from his phone."

"We can't use the video in court unless he gave you permission to take it."

Susan shook her head. "A private investigator got it for me."

"If there's more evidence on his phone, we should be able to get it legally through discovery. Same goes for his computer, paper records, anything that might be evidence."

"The investigator is digging around for more," Susan said. "Did you look into his assets? I'm sure he has accounts and properties I don't know about."

"I wouldn't go looking too deeply into those," Martin warned.

"Why not?"

"I reviewed the tax returns you sent me, and I did a little digging on my own. All I can say is... something doesn't add up. Will has a lot more money than he's reporting."

"So why shouldn't I look into it?"

"I have a bad feeling about it," Martin said.

Susan studied him for a moment, and then said, "OK. I'll leave that in your hands."

"Thank you, Susan."

* * *

Forty minutes later, as Martin and Susan were getting up to leave, Ready and Ella walked in. Ready was standing by the hostess' podium when he saw Susan across the room. "Oh, shit!"

"What?" asked Ella.

"I have to go to the bathroom. I'll be back in a minute."

Ready disappeared into the men's room a moment before Susan and her lawyer walked by. Susan dropped an envelope as they passed.

"Ma'am," Ella called, picking up the envelope. "Ma'am, you dropped this."

Susan turned and took the envelope. She was about to thank Ella when she recognized her from the video. Her eyes narrowed in anger, and she slapped Ella hard across the face and said, "Cunt!" Then she turned and left.

Ella stood staring after her in astonishment with her hand on her cheek and her mouth half open. When Ready returned a moment later, he asked, "Are you OK?"

"Oh my God!" Ella exclaimed. "I just met the rudest person ever!" As the hostess led them to a table, she continued. "Seriously! I did her a fucking favor and she slapped me in the face. What the fuck is her problem?"

"You never can tell what people are going through," Ready said. "You want a glass of wine? It might take the sting off your cheek."

Ready ordered a bottle of Chardonnay, and a few minutes later they were chatting at ease. "What would you do if you left Santa Barbara?" Ready asked.

"Probably go back to modeling."

"You like modeling?"

"Not really," said Ella. "But it's the only way I'll ever be able to pay for law school."

"Law school? Isn't that...hard?"

"Nothing's really that difficult if you find it interesting," she said. "What about you? What do you want to do?"

He shrugged. "I don't know."

"Have you ever thought of becoming a model? You have the looks for it."

He looked down at his lap and mumbled unintelligibly. "Oh, I... moooshoooo...."

Ella laughed. "What?"

Still looking down, Ready mumbled, "I'm not smart enough for that," but she didn't hear him.

"I don't think I've ever seen you so embarrassed," she laughed. "What's the matter, Warren? Are you shy?" She reached under the table and put her hand on his knee.

Ready looked up at her with a serious expression and nodded yes. This just made her laugh harder.

After the waitress took their order, Ella said, "I have your files. You wouldn't believe all the crap I found on Will's phone. He has a girlfriend in every city. He's got photos of thirty different women in there. And not one of his wife."

"How do you know what his wife looks like?" Ready asked.

"I don't," Ella said. "But I know she's forty. Will told me that. These women are all in their twenties. And they're all in bikinis or underwear, or they're naked. Men don't carry photos like that of their wives."

She paused for a moment, looking thoughtful and sad. "The women in the photos all look sad and vulnerable. Maybe it's just me projecting, but that's what I see. Are they sex workers? Did someone force them into this? Or were they just reckless like me?"

She looked directly at Ready, and said, "You know he's a predator. He chooses his targets. I'm so stupid. I knew what he was. I walked into this with my eyes open."

"Why?" Ready asked.

"I don't know," Ella said irritably. "Why do you drink so much when you know how sick it's going to make you? I wanted to do it. I did it on purpose."

She looked at him quietly for a moment, and then asked, "What do you think of me, Warren?"

"I think the world of you."

"What about when you first met me?"

"You came on a little strong. You scared me."

"I could tell. But then you came back. Why? For sex? Or for me?"

"I wanted to find the person I saw through the window—the graceful girl in white with the sweet voice."

"You like her?" Ella asked. "More than the crazy woman on the couch?"

"I like them both."

After a moment, Ella said, "You know what else? When I went through Will's computer...." She paused and tried to think of how to phrase her thought. "He's up to something. He didn't come by his money honestly. Not all of it."

"What do you mean?" Ready asked.

"He keeps two sets of books. He's got these spreadsheets that keep track of all the ships and what's on them and when they went through customs and how much he wound up selling everything for. But then he's got this other spreadsheet that describes some of the same shipments, with a different set of payments. There's no information about inventory, just two payments for each shipment. One before the ship leaves China, and one after it arrives in the US. Those payments come to almost two million dollars."

"What do you think he's doing?" Ready asked.

"Smuggling something," Ella replied. She thought for a moment, then added, "I kept thinking about his wife when I was looking at all those young women he runs around with. I feel bad for her. I couldn't imagine being married to Will. But I really started to get upset when I realized she'll lose everything if he gets in trouble. The IRS will seize his assets. She'll be left with nothing unless she can show she didn't know what was going on. You're his friend, Warren. Do you know his wife?"

"Yes," Ready said.

"Do you think she knows what goes on in his business?"

"I don't think so," Ready said.

"It's important that she doesn't," Ella said. "If the IRS gets to him, the only protection she has is innocent spouse relief, and she'll only get that if she really doesn't know what he's up to."

Ready marveled at her. "How do you know all this? You're like a lawyer."

"I told you that's what I'm going to be. I'm not going to spend my life smiling into a camera." She thought for a moment, then added, "You know what I'm going to do? I'm going to put together a disk with photos of all his little girlfriends, and all his texts and emails, and give that to his wife. I hope she divorces him."

She thought again then said, "Oh, but I can't do that. It would be cruel to throw all that in her face."

"His wife knows he's cheating," Ready said.

"She does?"

"Yeah. It might hurt her to see all the evidence, but it would help her get a divorce. That's what she wants."

Ella stared at him for several seconds with Susan's silent measuring gaze. In her eyes was a hardness he had not seen before, and he became uncomfortable.

"Is that why she hired you?" Ella asked.

"What?"

"Did Will's wife hire you to collect evidence of his affairs?"

Ready didn't know what to say as his discomfort sank into fear.

"Come on, Warren. You were peeping in my window. You carry pre-paid credit cards with no name on them. You asked me to steal files from Will's computer. I saw your website. It's the first thing that comes up when you Google Warren Lane. I know what you do."

She reflected for a moment then added, "It's funny. You're smart in some ways and clueless in others. You know how to keep a low profile. You have no photo on your website. No Facebook. No Tumblr, Instagram or Twitter. No LinkedIn. It's like you don't exist. And you got me to do all your dirty work. That was clever. But what if I hadn't been there? What would you have done? What if it had been some other woman? Would you have seduced her?"

"Excuse me?" said Ready. "Did I seduce you?"

Ella looked down at her lap and said, "You didn't have to." She looked back up at him with a hint of fear and said, "I don't know if you'll go away, or if you really care for me, but I'll give you the files, Warren. And I'm going to write a note for his wife to go with them. Will you give it to her?"

"Yes," Ready said.

"That poor woman." Ella sighed. "It might sound strange, but I feel like I should look out for her. I know I'd take her side over his if it came to a fight. And here I am, sleeping with the man she loves. I feel awful about that. I'm horrible, Warren. Horrible!"

She put her hand to her cheek and let out a little laugh. "Maybe it was karma."

"What was karma?"

"That slap in the face. I deserve that, and a lot more."

"There's probably a simpler explanation," Ready said.

Ella's face brightened, and she said, "Warren? What if I printed out some of those spreadsheets from Will's computer? You could go to him and ask for some money. You know, to keep quiet."

"What?" Ready exclaimed with a look of shock. "Extortion? No!"

"I know. It was just a thought," said Ella. "It's not that I want to hurt him. I just want to get out of this life I'm in. If we had some money, we could go away and start a real life. Just you and me."

Ready looked down at his lap.

"What's wrong? Wouldn't you like to run away with me?"

"I don't know," he said. Ready avoided thinking about the future, with its prospects of commitment and responsibility. It was that same old fear of his: if he were to let someone close enough to truly see him, he would be exposed as unworthy and then abandoned. By avoiding hope, he avoided disappointment.

He regretted his response, and was ashamed of himself for allowing his fears to prevent him from saying yes to what he knew he wanted. He dreaded looking up and seeing how his hesitation disappointed her. He expected to see in her face some recognition of his cowardice, and to read in her expression the thought, *If you don't think you're worth my time, why should I bother with you?* But when he raised his gaze to meet her open face, he found her clear, bright eyes looking warmly back at him.

"Thank you for being honest with me, Warren," she said simply. "It means a lot to me."

Her acceptance of the doubt he had been ashamed to confess now loosened the final restraint on his heart, and he began to fall. She knew this, though he did not. Looking into his eyes, Ella thought, *We will be together, you and I. One day you will love me as much as I love you. It's only a matter of time.*

Chapter 21

The following morning, Warren Lane strolled casually into the restoration room in the basement of the art museum. The soft leather soles of his shoes made almost no sound on the concrete floor as he approached the restoration artist.

"Good morning, Mrs. DiBiase," he said.

"You can call me Sophie," the woman replied as she shook his hand. She was thin, in her late forties, and her dark hair was tied in a bun on top of her head. She wore a white smock, and he could feel the bones in her long, slim fingers.

Looking around at the paintings and sculptures in various phases of restoration, Lane said in a friendly tone, "Makes me a little nervous to be in here with all this priceless art just sitting out in the open. I'm afraid I might bump into something and break it."

"Oh," Sophie smiled. "These works aren't priceless. Some of them are expensive though. That one," she said, pointing to a small Roman statue, "is a actually a reproduction. A very good reproduction. One of our staff broke its pinky off during a move."

"Ooh," said Lane, wincing as is he felt the pain himself.

Maxine had once remarked that watching Lane talk to a woman was like watching a dog walk on its hind legs. It was amusing at first, but after a few minutes, you just wanted the unnatural act to stop. Maxine coached him on some basic manners, but kindness and decency were not native to him, and he was unable to express them with grace or ease. Instead, he came off as overly polite, while inwardly he chafed at the constraints of civility, like a thirteen-year-old boy whose mother had stuffed him into his Sunday School suit when he'd rather be out torturing cats.

"It's not that bad," Sophie said with a little laugh. "I've fixed worse. What can I help you with?"

"I came across an article the other day, just a little blurb really, about an exhibit from last year."

"Which one was that?" Sophie asked.

"A Chinese dynasty... um... The article said that a large urn had shattered during shipment."

"Yes, that was sad."

"Any idea how that might have happened?"

"Rough seas? I don't know. It really didn't make any sense to me. It was still in its crate when it arrived at the museum. I don't see how it could have shattered in that packaging."

"Moore Imports handled the shipping and logistics?"

"Yes. We work with them periodically. His wife is a patron of the museum. She's helped us raise quite a bit of money."

"She sounds like a fine woman. Where did that urn go?"

"Oh, it was beyond repair. Most of it went back to China. But we sent a few pieces out to labs and universities."

"What would they want with a broken urn?"

"It's not what they want. It's what we want. We want to know what the glazes and dyes are made of. They vary from century to century and from region to region."

"You have a very interesting job, Mrs. DiBiase," said Lane gratuitously, and forced what he hoped was a friendly smile. "Did you learn anything new from that urn?"

"Not really," Sophie said. "It just confirmed some things we knew already." She paused a moment to recall a detail from the lab reports, then added, "But there was one weird thing."

"What's that?" Lane asked.

"All of the labs said they found traces of bleach inside the urn. No one ever cleans those pieces with bleach. I mean, no one in the art world."

"Why would someone pour bleach into an ancient urn?" Lane asked.

"It's beyond me," Sophie replied.

"Unless they're trying to wash away all traces of its contents."

"Oh, those urns are just decorative," Sophie said. "No one puts anything in them, especially during shipment."

Chapter 22

That afternoon, Ready was back at Susan's hotel. "Just a minute," she said in response to his knock. She cracked the door open as far as it would go before the little sliding chain stopped it. Ready could see one side of her wet face and the towel wrapped around her hair.

"Oh, hi, Warren. Can you give me a minute to get dressed?"

"Sure," he said.

Susan watched him through the crack for just a second longer than he liked. He was amazed at how that one dark eye could at once be so inviting and so intimidating. She shut the door and slid the chain out of its little track. The door opened all the way and there she stood, dripping wet and wrapped in a towel.

"Mrs. Moore?" said Ready nervously.

"Come in," she said, smiling at his discomfort.

She didn't give him space to pass, and he could feel the moist heat of the shower radiating from her skin as he brushed by. He went to the far end of the room and looked out the window. Susan picked up her clothes from the bed and took them into the bathroom, where she dressed with the door open.

She returned to the room a minute later and asked, "Do you have something for me, Warren?"

"Um...." He looked fixedly out the window.

"Warren, I'm dressed. You can turn around."

Ready turned slowly and pulled a little USB drive from his pocket. "Mrs. Moore, I have the files you want on this drive."

"Why are you calling me Mrs. Moore?" she asked. "You know my name is Susan."

"Why do you answer the door in a towel?" Ready asked. "You know you're married."

"That didn't stop you from kissing me last time we met."

"That was a mistake."

"Was it?"

Ready shrugged, and for the first time he examined her the way she had so often examined him. She did not shrink from it or show any of the discomfort that he felt under her scrutiny.

She said, "When I texted you the other day to ask when we could meet, you texted back, 'Will you be naked?' What am I supposed to make of that?"

"I'm sorry," Ready said. "Things in my world are a little confused right now."

"Mine too," Susan sighed. "I'm not even the same person from one minute to the next."

"I know. I feel it when I'm around you."

"And it makes you nervous," Susan said.

"It does. After I left our last meeting, I kept asking myself what the hell just happened."

"So did I. What do you have there?" Susan nodded toward the USB stick. "Are we going to watch some more porn?"

"No," said Ready, looking a little glum. "I don't really know how to say this, so I'll just say it. Your husband is having several affairs."

Susan took a deep breath and looked at him calmly. "OK," she said.

"And these women are all very young."

"That doesn't surprise me," Susan said, maintaining her calmness with visible effort.

"I just want to warn you that some of these photos are...well, there are a lot of them. I'm just letting you know now, so you're prepared."

Susan, now trembling slightly, nodded to indicate she understood.

"There are emails and texts in there too," Ready said. "It might be better just to let the lawyers read those. Your whole case is right here, Susan."

"OK," Susan said. Her voice was beginning to break, but she held on tightly to her composure.

"And there's one more thing," Ready added, pulling Ella's note from his pocket. "I want you to read this. It has some important information to protect you from the IRA."

"The Irish Republican Army?" Susan asked.

Ready looked at the note. "IRS?"

"May I see that?" Susan asked. Ready handed her the note. In a broad, looping hand, it read:

Mrs. Moore,

In the course of our investigation, we have discovered some troubling implications in your husband's business records. If your divorce goes to court, your tax returns and other financial documents may come under examination as you battle over alimony and division of assets.

Without giving away anything more, we ask you to avoid looking too far into your husband's finances. Do not discuss business matters with him. There will come a time when your ignorance of his activities will be what saves you. For now, leave all matters of discovery to your attorneys, and follow their advice.

Please destroy this note.

There was no signature. Susan turned the paper over. The other side was blank. She turned it back again, and then looked at Ready in bewilderment and asked, "What is this?"

"I can't tell you any more than what it says there," Ready said.

"What has Will been doing?"

"I don't know exactly," Ready said. "But I wouldn't tell you if I did know."

"Does this mean he's going to jail? Is he going to leave me with nothing?" Ready felt her rising fear and was afraid, both for her welfare and at how her distress affected him.

"I don't know," he said. "I don't know what it means." He wished Ella were there to explain everything. He tried to remember her words. "Your part is just to stay out of his business. That's all you have to do."

These words calmed her, and she looked again at the letter.

"You didn't write this, did you Warren?"

"Why do you say that?"

"This is a woman's handwriting. And I don't think you're capable of composing these kinds of sentences."

"Oh," Ready said proudly. "My assistant wrote that. She's really sharp."

"So I see," Susan said. She scanned through the note again, and then said, "Thank you, Warren. Thank you for doing all this for me."

She kissed him softly on the cheek. After starting to draw away, he pulled her in and kissed her on the mouth. Then he stared at her for a second in confusion and said, "Susan, I really have to go. I can't stay here with you."

He turned and left without looking back, and she watched after him with a smile.

After he left, she filled the coffee maker and turned the switch on. She read the note again as the coffee maker gurgled, then tore it up and flushed the pieces down the toilet.

She poured a cup of coffee and inserted the USB drive into her laptop. There she saw the four folders into which Ella had neatly arranged everything: Photos, Emails, Texts, and Travel.

There was also a document. Susan opened it to see neatly laid out tables showing the correlations between the dates of the photos, emails, texts, and travel:

April 2: Email to Hitomi
April 9,10,11: Texts to Hitomi
April 11: Flight to Tokyo
April 12-14: At Tokyo Hilton
April 12: Photo of Hitomi in restaurant
April 12: Photo of Hitomi in hotel room in underwear

The document went on like this for many pages.

Susan opened the photos folder and was shocked by the sheer number of images. She clicked on a picture of a young Thai woman standing under a palm tree wearing only a pink bikini bottom. Her left arm was folded across her chest, and the expression on her face showed she didn't want to be photographed.

"Good God, Will! How old is that one? Eighteen?"

She browsed through a few more photos, studying each of the women and comparing herself to them. "He likes them young," she observed. "And skinny."

After the first dozen or so, she raced through the remaining photos, spending less and less time on each woman. Her breath became more shallow and rapid as the parade of images overwhelmed her. She felt a new revulsion for her husband, deeper than anything she had felt before. Her disgust mixed with feelings of anger, betrayal, abandonment and nausea.

She stood up abruptly from the computer when her last click brought Ella's sweetly smiling face to the screen. The photo showed just her head and shoulders, the blue straps of her bikini standing out against the light-brown slats of a poolside chair.

As much as it shamed her to do it, Ella had included Will's photos of herself, along with their texts and emails. Her sense of duty to this injured woman compelled her to be completely honest.

"Oh, you!" Susan said. "You nasty little slut! If I ever see you again, I'll slit your fucking throat!" Ella had almost the same feelings when she first came across this photo among Will's trove of images.

Susan slammed the laptop shut and spent the next ten minutes pacing her hotel room, crying and shuddering.

Chapter 23

The following morning, Will was at his desk when his phone rang.

"Hello?" said Will.

"Hey, Will. It's Arnie."

"Oh, good timing," Will said. "I was just finishing up some work for the quarterly books. If expenses are close to last quarter, we're doing well."

"Expenses are about the same," Arnie said, "but that's not what I'm calling about."

"What's up?"

"Something strange happened last night. I went into the office around midnight, and saw a guy leaving the building. Inside the office some of the drawers were open, and some things were out of place. The alarm hadn't gone off, and when I checked the security station, all of the cameras had been shut off. This guy knew what he was doing."

"Sounds like it," Will said.

"But here's the weird thing. He got into my assistant's computer, and he left what he was looking at right there on the screen. Like he wanted us to know what he was after. It was your stuff, Will. Payroll, accounts, taxes. It was all up there on the screen. He probably copied the files."

"You say you saw the guy coming out of the building?"

"Yeah."

"What did he look like?"

"Skinny guy. Maybe around forty," said Arnie.

"Got a beak for a nose and hair combed straight back?"

"Yeah. You know him?"

"Yeah, I know that little piece of shit."

"Sorry to be the bearer of bad news, Will."

"No, no. I appreciate you telling me."

"You'll send me those files today?" Arnie asked.

"I'll have 'em to you in an hour or so."

Will hung up and put his feet up on his desk. "Warren Lane," he said slowly. "You are starting to get under my skin."

Chapter 24

While Will was talking to his accountant, Lane was arriving at his office with a cup of coffee. Maxine was at her desk, leaning forward, her face just a few inches from her computer monitor.

"Find anything interesting in there?" Lane asked.

"Yes I did," she said. "There's a spreadsheet in here showing deposits and transfers from an account labeled 'HK.' It's all hand-entered data. Look at this."

Lane took a seat at the edge of her desk, and she turned the monitor so he could see it. "Looks promising," he said.

"There's more," Maxine said. "Every deposit into this HK account happens the day before a shipping container leaves China or a few days after it clears customs in Long Beach. Look." She pulled up another spreadsheet showing container numbers, manifest summaries, and shipping dates. "It's not every shipment. Only once every few months he gets these payments. One hundred thousand when the ship leaves China. Two hundred thousand after it arrives in the US. The first few shipments were fifty thousand for the initial payment. But it went up a few months ago."

"That *is* interesting," said Lane, looking excited. "This is the part of the job I love. Keep digging. Let me know what you find."

Chapter 25

Ready returned to Susan's hotel late that afternoon, the day after he'd given her the flash drive. He knocked on the door.

"Who is it?" Susan asked. Her voice sounded flat.

"It's Warren."

When Ready heard the chain sliding on the inside of the door, he asked, "Are you dressed?"

Susan opened the door and looked him in the face. "I'm dressed," she said. Her hair was a mess, and he could see she had been crying.

"May I come in?" he asked.

She stepped aside to let him by and closed the door behind him.

"I just wanted to check on you," Ready said. He studied her drained face. "I know what you saw yesterday must have hurt."

Susan made no response. She just stared at him blankly, her eyes distant and unfocused.

"Did you sleep last night?"

She shook her head slowly. "No."

"You should sit down," said Ready. "You don't look well."

He guided her to the edge of the bed and they both sat down.

"Have you eaten?" he asked.

She shook her head. "I'm not hungry." She lay down and curled onto her side and put her head on the pillow.

"Can I get you some coffee?"

She shook her head.

"Do you want me to leave?"

"No. I'm glad you're here. I'm tired of being alone with my thoughts."

She closed her eyes, and let her mind drift. When she opened them a few seconds later, Ready was staring at her.

"You don't like it when I stare at you like that," she said with a little smile.

"Sorry," Ready said.

Susan sat up and put her arms around his neck. "You do make me feel better, you know. And it's not just because you think about me and check in on me. It's just...you." She kissed him, and he returned her kiss with passion.

Her smiled broadened, though it was still tinged with sadness. She ran her hand down his chest and stomach, following it with her eyes. Looking up from his pants, she said, "Oh, Warren, I can't do that right now. I just can't."

"I wouldn't ask you to. I think you need to get out. You need some air."

Susan nodded. "You're right."

"I'll take you up to the mountains," Ready said. "I know a nice, short hike. Do you think you're up to it?"

"Yes, I think so."

"Good answer," Ready said. "All joy begins with yes. Grab your shoes."

"All I have are these," Susan said, picking up a pair of flats near the closet.

"It's a ten minute hike. You'll be fine in those."

Ready took a seat at the desk, where he laid a little packet next to the lamp and began to roll up a dollar bill.

"What are you doing?" Susan asked.

"Just a little pick-me-up," Ready said. "I'm a little slow today, too."

"What *is* that?" Susan said, snatching the packet from the desk.

"Just a little coke," Ready said.

Susan put the package into the pocket of her skirt.

"What are you doing?" Ready asked.

"Saving your life. Is this what you did with the money I gave you?"

Ready shrugged. "It's just a little treat I enjoy now and then."

"No," said Susan. "You need to stop this. Half the time I see you, you're hung over. You need to get a hold of yourself."

Ready turned away from her and looked angrily out the window.

Susan walked around him and looked him in the eye. "You can't keep doing this, Warren. You're a beautiful person, but you're killing yourself, and it breaks my heart."

"That packet's not sealed," Ready said. "It's going to leak."

"So what?" Susan said. "I'm going to throw it out as soon as we leave."

"That cost a lot of money," Ready said.

"I don't care. I'm getting rid of it."

Susan put her shoes on. When they got on the elevator they found the control panel hanging from the wall and Omar standing in front of it.

"Hey, Warren."

"Hey, Omar. This is Susan." She shook his hand.

"Nice to meet you," Omar said.

"Nice to meet you," Susan said. "Are you two friends?"

"We drank some beers together once," said Omar. "You want the lobby?"

"Yes, please," Susan said.

Omar picked up the control panel and pressed L.

In the lobby, Susan headed for the coffee shop and Ready said, "Meet me in front in a few minutes. I'll pull the car around."

Chapter 26

Warren Lane was leaving a meeting on the second floor of the hotel when his phone rang.

"Warren, I was just going through the payroll records and I think I found your man," Maxine said. "Moore's got an hourly worker named Yun Zhu. Looks like he does some janitorial work, packing, and unloading. Every time one of those shipments comes in with the big payment attached, this guy clocks in around 10:00 p.m. and works until two or three in the morning. And that's after he's worked a full day."

"OK," said Lane.

"It gets better," Maxine said.

"Ooh. I'm getting excited."

"His social security number belongs to a guy who died a few years ago."

"Interesting."

"I think he's illegal."

"Where does he live?"

"LA. I have his address."

"Sounds like it's time for a little drive," said Lane.

He ended the call just as he was exiting the hotel. And there in front of him was an unexpected sight.

As a valet pulled up in his red Audi with the broken driver side mirror, Susan turned to see Lane's sharp green eyes staring through her. She instantly marked him as a psychopath. He approached her with the graceful ease of a tiger, and she could not suppress a little smile at his arrogance.

"Susan Moore," Lane said. He rudely looked her up and down, appraising her as if she were a horse, and pausing pointedly at her breasts and thighs. She understood he was trying to intimidate her, but there was something odd about the man—something asexual, stunted, and almost pre-adolescent. "I have a message for your husband," Lane said.

Susan said nothing.

"You know he's been doing a little business on the side. It's not just pretty pictures and nice furniture he's importing."

He lifted a lock of hair from her shoulder and rubbed it between his fingers. "Have you ever wondered how he affords that big house? Those fine cars? All the travel?"

He looked into her eyes and saw to his surprise that she was still at ease. Her lips were fixed in a faint, curious smile. Lane decided to bring out his next weapon.

"Or the other house? How does he afford that? You know about his other house, don't you? With his other woman? The little blonde?"

Still her eyes were calm and the smile remained.

"I don't know why he'd need another woman when he has you at home, as pretty as you are," Lane said. He inched back to look her over once more, this time examining the line of her back. He put his hand on her shoulder, turning her slightly to get a look at her behind. "But you're getting older, I suppose. Perhaps the mileage is starting to show. Maybe you're not as pretty with your dress off as you are with it on. It's always a shame when a woman reaches that age."

In her mind, she confirmed her initial judgment of him. She saw no ring on his finger, and she wondered for a moment if he had ever kissed a woman.

"Or maybe you're just frigid," he said.

She turned and put her hand gently on his cheek, pulled his face toward hers, and kissed him on the mouth. As she did this, she slipped the leaking packet of cocaine into the front pocket of his jacket.

When she drew away, she saw the confident tiger transformed into a startled housecat. Warren Lane had no idea what to make of what just happened. Her smile broadened just slightly when Ready's blue Toyota approached the curb.

She got into Ready's car, and Lane, still puzzled, turned to look at her before getting into his Audi. The two cars left the hotel simultaneously, and Lane sped off. Susan pulled out her phone and dialed 911. "I'd like to report a drunk driver," she said. "Red Audi.... Yes, I have the license number."

After she hung up, Ready asked, "What was that all about?"

"I don't know," Susan said.

"It seems to have perked you up."

"I don't like people like that," Susan said. "But it's nice to have the chance to be nasty to someone and not feel bad about it."

A few minutes later, they saw Lane's Audi at the side of the road, parked in front of a police cruiser with flashing lights. Ready slowed his Toyota and Susan smiled and waved her fingers. Lane watched them as they passed.

When the policeman appeared beside his window, Lane said, "What's the problem, officer?"

"License and registration, please," the officer said flatly.

Lane handed him the documents and said, "I know your supervisor."

"I hope I can tell him we had a pleasant meeting," the policeman replied. "What happened to your mirror here?"

"It seems to have broken off, officer," Lane said with a subtle hint of mockery. "Couldn't you tell? You were looking right at it."

"Step out of the car," said the cop.

"What?"

"Step out of the car."

"Oh, I don't think that will be necessary."

"Get out of the goddamn car!" the policeman commanded.

Lane opened the door and climbed out.

"Have you been drinking?"

"Not at all, officer," Lane said with smile. "You can give me a breathalyzer if you'd like. I'm not a drinker."

"What's this?" the officer asked.

"What's what?" said Lane.

"This trail of white powder on your jacket." As Lane looked down, the policeman wiped a bit the powder off and rubbed it between his fingers.

"That looks like cocaine," the policeman said. He pulled the packet from Lane's pocket.

Lane was about to protest, but instead he laughed as he realized how Susan had got the better of him.

"You think this is funny?" said the officer, twisting Lane's arm and spinning him roughly around.

"Watch the suit, you fucking ape!"

"Shut the fuck up!" the cop replied. He clapped the cuffs on, and stuffed him into the back of the cruiser.

Chapter 27

An hour later, Ready and Susan approached a stony clearing at the top of the mountain. They were breathing heavily.

"See," Ready said. "It wasn't that hard."

"That was more than ten minutes," Susan said.

"Yeah, but we're here."

Susan looked out at the broad vista before them, where the narrow strip of Route 1 traced the edge of the shining Pacific. At the southern edge of Santa Barbara, the road drifted inland and the traffic snaked silently through the turn at the harbor.

"I come up here sometimes when I need some perspective," Ready said as they sat on a rock.

"You come up with your friends?"

"No," Ready said. "I don't really have any friends."

"Why not?"

Ready shrugged. "They've all moved on. They have jobs and stuff."

"You have a job," Susan said.

"Kind of. But I'm not sitting in an office from nine to five. And some of my friends moved to different cities. Some of them are getting married. Our lives aren't the same anymore."

"You look sad when you say that."

"Do I?" He thought for a moment. "Sometimes I don't know where my life is going. I heard this song on the radio the other day. *Running on Empty.*"

"Jackson Browne," Susan said.

"Is that who sings it? It describes my life."

The two of them sat watching the city in silence. After a while, Ready said, "You see how small the city is from here? It seems big when we're in it, but from up here, it's just a little spot in a very big world. And all our troubles are wrapped up in there. In that little place." He drew a circle around the city with his finger.

"That's poetic, Warren. You surprise me."

"Because you think I'm dumb."

"I never said that."

"You did. You said it with your eyes the first time we met. And you said it when you asked if I'd ever thought of modeling."

"I don't really think you're stupid," Susan said. "I mean, you have to admit, you have your moments. Like when you looked at my dress and called it a skirt."

"That was just nerves," Ready said. "I was hung over, and you were measuring me with that stare of yours."

"I do stare," Susan said. "It puts people off sometimes."

"People have made those insinuations my whole life," Ready said. "'Oh, there's the good-looking kid who's not too bright. Maybe he'll be an actor someday.' When you hear that enough times, you start to believe it. You're one of those pretty, hollow shells little girls pick up on the beach."

"Warren, I'm sorry if I made you feel that way," Susan said.

"Gets me laid a lot though."

"I believe it."

"A lot!"

"I get it, Warren."

"How are you holding up?" Ready asked.

"OK right now. I'm mostly just tired. But it's good to be out in the air and sun. I'm glad you brought me here." Susan paused, then added, "I had lunch with my lawyer the other day."

"How'd that go?" Ready asked.

"Good and bad. I mean, he said we'd be in good shape if we could get more evidence from Will's phone or his computer. And then you brought me plenty of that. But that stuff was hard to look at, Warren. It really hurt. And the lawyers will have to get it all again, legally, through discovery." She paused a moment, as if reviewing the images again in her mind. "I'm going to leave him. I didn't ever think it would be this hard, but I have to do it."

"Do you ever waver?"

"Sometimes. But I know it's over. You know, my lawyer hinted at the same thing as the note you gave me. He told me he thought Will's been doing things that could bring us a lot of trouble. But I'm just trying to keep my head out of all that right now. I have so much on my mind already. It's hard to leave a life you've lived for so long. Even when you really want to."

"I know," Ready said.

Susan looked him in the eyes and nodded. "I thought you would."

Ready turned away from her and picked up a handful of stones and threw them down the mountain one at a time. For the next few minutes, he wouldn't look at her.

"You want to start walking back?" he asked, after the last stone was gone.

"We just got here," Susan said.

"I want to go," Ready said.

"Did I upset you?"

Ready got up and started back toward the car without answering her.

"That's it?" Susan asked. "We're leaving?" He still didn't respond, so she got up and walked after him.

Forty minutes later, they were still walking. Susan was several steps behind him, carrying her shoes. Her face was red as she asked with annoyance and frustration, "Where is the car, Warren? I thought you said you've been here before."

"I have," said Ready. "Just not on this trail."

"Well why don't you stick to the trails you know? Why did you drag me out here? You know I haven't slept. And now I'm hot, and I'm tired, and I'm hungry. My feet hurt, and you can't even find the fucking car."

He turned and said, "I'm trying, OK? I'm doing my best."

"Goddammit, Warren," she said, struggling to control her frustration. "You're a kind man, and you're a good man, and I would hold on to you forever if only you had a fucking brain in your head."

He froze and she instantly regretted her words. She was about to apologize when he said, "That's one of nicest things anyone has ever said to me."

"That you have no brain?"

"That you'd hold on to me forever."

Disarmed by his response, her frustration melted away. She kissed him and held his hand for the next few minutes until they found the car.

They drove straight back to the hotel, and she looked anxious and forlorn when he dropped her off. He felt guilty leaving her alone, but he wanted to drink.

"Don't you want to come up to the room?" Susan asked.

"No," Ready said. "I have some things to do."

She thought of asking again, but instead she said, "OK, Warren. Take care of yourself. And thank you."

Ready drove to the sports bar and planted himself in front of the taps. Two hours later, Omar arrived.

"Man, you're already drunk," Omar said.

"I'm working on it," said Ready.

"Hey, that woman in the elevator... she the one that hired you?"

"She's the one," Ready said. "Her name is Susan."

"She's pretty. You didn't tell me that part. A pretty married woman in trouble?" Omar shook his head. "You're askin' for trouble man. Just beggin' for it."

Ready shrugged.

"You two, uh…?"

"No," said Ready. "I'm seeing someone else."

"Who?" Omar asked.

"Her husband's mistress."

Omar stared at him for a moment, then shook his head and said, "You're just about as dumb as I thought you were. You'll probably be snorting blow in another hour."

"Probably," said Ready. "You want a beer?"

"Sure."

Four beers later, Ready was back at Larry's buying more cocaine. An hour after that, he was at Ella's. She chastised him for showing up without calling first. "Will could have been here," she said. "He sometimes comes by after work."

"Is he coming tonight?" Ready asked.

"No."

"Can I stay?"

"Yes."

Chapter 28

The next morning, Ella stood at the stove, mixing eggs in a bowl, while a pan of sautéed mushrooms cooled on the back burner. Beside the eggs were a bowl of fresh spinach and a package of feta cheese. Ella turned on the burner beneath a frying pan.

"How much did you drink last night?" she asked without turning around. "You look awful."

Ready sat at the counter with his head in his hands. "I don't know," he said. "Too much."

"I wish you'd stop that, Warren. Do you need to go back to bed? Because if you do, you'll have to go home. Will's coming today."

Ready groaned and searched through his pockets until he found the packet of cocaine and a little straw. He opened the packet on the counter, snorted from it directly, then jerked his head back and said, "Whoa. Too much."

Ella turned from the stove to look at him. "What the hell are you doing?" she asked.

"Trying to wake up," Ready said. "But I got too much."

"Get out. You cannot do that in this house. Leave, Warren! Now!" She looked more hurt than angry.

"Are you serious?"

"Yes, I'm fucking serious."

Ready closed up the packet of cocaine and put it back in his pocket.

"I'm sorry," Ella said angrily. "Your drinking is bad enough, but *that* I just won't have."

"My drinking?" Ready said as he stood to go. "You have a problem with my drinking?"

"*You* have a problem with your drinking," Ella said. Ready started toward the door and Ella followed.

"So what are you going to do? Make me stop? Are you going to take control of that part of my life too?"

"*You* need to take control of your life," Ella corrected.

"Just like you took control of my car and my phone and got rid of everything you didn't like?"

Ella grabbed his elbow and turned him around. "Do you want your women back? Do you want me to put the trash back in your car? Would your life be better then? Would it, Warren?"

"Fuck you," he muttered just loud enough for her to hear as he walked out the door.

He got into his car and started the engine. His heart was beating fast from the cocaine, and his top front teeth were going numb. When he released the parking brake, Ella was knocking at his window. He rolled it down.

"What?" he asked.

Ella looked scared and uncertain, and her words came pouring out: "I know I can be pushy, Warren, and maybe that's not the right way to be. But it's only because I want this to work. I really do! And I don't want to compete with your drugs, and I don't want just the half of you that's here when you're drunk. If you give me all of you, Warren, I'll give you all of me. I'll give you everything."

All he could say before he drove away was, "Sorry." Even more than her words, her earnestness pierced his heart. He was flooded with shame to know he was being offered what he so badly wanted but was not prepared to receive.

Ella understood this and forgave him. When she got back into the house, she texted him. "I'm not mad. Come back when you're sober."

On the way home, Ready convinced himself that a drink would calm his shaking hands and soothe his racing heart. He arrived at the house with a twelve-pack of beer and a bottle of bourbon. By early afternoon, the house was spinning and he was full of hatred for himself. By three o'clock, he was unconscious.

Chapter 29

At eleven the following morning, Ella answered her phone on the first ring. "Hello?"

"Can I come over?" Ready asked.

"Are you sober?"

"I am."

"You can come over if you promise to drink nothing today. And no drugs."

"OK," Ready said. "What have you been doing?"

Ella was silent for a moment. "Waiting for you to call."

"Really? That's sweet."

"No, it's not," Ella said. "It's pathetic."

"Ella?"

"What?" Her tone was short and impatient.

"I won't let you down."

"You better not."

"Ella?"

"What?"

"I don't deserve you."

"You don't?" Ella asked with a sharp edge to her voice. "You don't deserve the girl who tricks you into taking off your clothes at the bottom of the stairs and then teases you? You totally deserve me, Warren."

When he arrived half an hour later, Ella didn't greet him with her usual warmth. Instead, she said impatiently, "Let's go somewhere. I want to get out of this house."

"Do you want to take a walk?" Ready asked.

"Fine. Come upstairs and keep me company while I change. I won't play any tricks this time."

Upstairs, Ready sat on the bed and watched Ella change into a pair of jeans. Neither of them spoke. She stood in front of the mirror for a long time, putting on one pair of earrings after another, turning her head from side to side and examining her reflection.

"We're just going for a walk," Ready said. "Why can't you just pick a pair?"

She turned on him with startling ferocity, and in a breaking voice she yelled, "Because I'm fucking lost! Can't you see that? I'm just as lost as you are, Warren! What kind of woman gets stuck in a house like this with a man twice her age? What kind of woman starts fucking a stranger who shows up at her window before she even asks his name? Do you think that's normal, Warren? Because if you do, you're even more fucked up than I am."

Then, calming a bit, she said, "Can't you see we're just two versions of the same person? Neither one of us knows what we're doing. Neither one of us knows where we're going. I deliberately missed my flight because I recognized you and I didn't want to abandon you. I'm going to get out of here, with you or without you." And then in a softer tone, she said, "But I want to do it with you. My offer stands: I will give you everything if you just say yes."

"Why?"

"Because I know you'll give me everything too."

"But I have nothing to give," Ready said.

"That's the alcohol talking."

"I haven't had anything to drink," Ready said.

"You don't need a drink to feel worthless. You feel it all the time, don't you, Warren?"

Ready said nothing.

"It scares you when I tell you I love you, doesn't it?"

Still he did not speak.

"Does it make me sound desperate? Well, I *am* desperate. And so are you. It scares you to think of having someone else's heart in your hands when you can't even manage your own life. I know it, Warren, because I'm just like you. What scares me most is that I know I'll walk out of here for good someday very soon. And if you're not there with me, I'll go alone. I'm growing up, Warren, and I hope I can do it with you. But I don't know if you're going to make it. I don't know how bad off you really are."

They were quiet for a moment. Ella angrily thrust her feet into a pair of running shoes and said, "Come on. Let's go for a walk."

She left the room and started down the stairs without waiting for him. He caught up to her at the front door, but a moment later she was ahead of him again. She marched for thirty minutes like this, Ready repeatedly falling behind and trotting to catch up. They did not speak.

When they returned to the house, their faces were red from exertion. Ella went up to the bedroom and took off her shoes. For the next hour, she lay on the bed, looking unhappily at the ceiling while Ready sat alone on the couch downstairs.

At the end of the hour, he brought her a glass of ice water. She was lying on her side, staring out the window. "I brought you this," he said.

"Did you get my text?" Ella asked.

"What text?"

"I asked you for ice water."

"No," Ready said. He pushed the button on his phone, but the screen didn't come on. "My battery is dead."

Ella took the glass from him and drank half of it at once. She pointed toward the dresser. "You can plug it in over there. The white cord is the charger."

Ready plugged in his phone, and then lay on his back on the bed next to her. He flipped through the pages of a magazine.

"I thought you didn't read those," Ella said.

"If I can't drink, I'll need to find a new hobby," Ready said.

Ella put the glass on the night table and lay her head on his chest. She was tired. She listened to the pages turning every two seconds above her head and said, "You can't really be reading that."

"I'm looking at the pictures."

"Do you even know how to read?" she asked in her playful, mocking tone. "I'll teach you. Then you'll be able to ride the bus all by yourself."

"What's the point of this magazine?" Ready asked, ignoring her teasing.

"Sell clothes."

Ready stopped flipping the pages and settled on an article. Ella drifted to sleep, and woke a few minutes later to see the magazine lying on the bed.

"Warren," she said.

"What?"

"Your thoughts are bothering you."

"How do you know?"

"Because your breathing is shallow, and your heart is beating fast. Are you afraid of Will showing up?"

"No. I'm afraid of you going away."

Ella lifted her head from his chest. She looked up at his face, put her finger to her lips, and said, "Shhh." Then she laid her head back on his heart.

"Will you go away?" Ready asked.

"Yes," she said. "Will you come with me?"

"Yes."

Chapter 30

While Ready and Ella lay together, Susan sat alone in her hotel room. She hadn't slept in two nights, although she'd napped briefly during the days. Her anxiety had begun to rise when she and Ready were driving back from their hike the day before, and she had feared this time alone.

She spent hours second-guessing her decision to marry Will. She reevaluated a thousand little memories, seeing each one anew in the light of her resentment and mistrust. The traits she used to admire in him now took on a more sinister cast. His confidence, his generosity, the way he could bring people around to his point of view—these were all now evidence of his manipulative and dissembling nature. She directed all her hatred and anger at him, and the more she tore him down, the more she hurt.

After anger came grief, the most painful of all emotions. She could not turn it outward, like anger and hatred, nor did it diminish as she grew tired. It was a merciless, relentless pain that forced her to feel more deeply than she could bear, even when she was too exhausted to endure any more. When it came, it possessed her completely. The magnitude and intensity of it filled her with the same sense of helplessness and physical terror she had felt as a child, when she fell from the tree and had the breath knocked out of her and couldn't move or breathe.

After grief came numbness and exhaustion, followed again by second-guessing and fear, and the dread of knowing that was she was entering another round of what she had just been through. With no parents or siblings to connect her to her past, and no children to brighten her future, she felt the full weight of her isolation, and she could see no way out of her suffering.

She blamed herself for the decisions she made in her twenties, when so much of her life was still before her. She blamed herself for not going back to school and for not establishing a career.

This is my own fault, she told herself as she paced the room in her delirium. *And now what? What if Will really is doing something illegal? What if he leaves me with nothing? What skills do I have? Who's going to give me a job? Oh, why did I stop seeing my friends? Where are they now? And why didn't you have kids? What are you going to do, Susan? How could you fuck up your life like this? You fucked it all up, and now you're alone with nowhere to go.*

When she caught a glimpse of herself in the mirror, her spirits were lifted momentarily, and she turned instinctively to look for reassurance in the reflection of that woman she had always known to be intelligent, resourceful, warm and deep.

But the reflection that greeted her was tired, weak and empty. The plea for help in the eyes of the woman on the other side of the glass irked her, and she said aloud, "Don't ask *me* for help. I have nothing to give you. Nothing!"

The pearl was gone now, and only the wound remained. In these hours alone, what she desired most was some kindness, some reassurance, some forgiveness from a spirit more generous than her own for whatever part she had played in making her life what it was.

She saw her fingers on the phone, but she didn't recognize them as her own, nor did she know who she was calling. Then the sound of Ready's voice at the other end of the line lifted her spirit once again, though only for a moment. "Hey, I'm not here," said the recording. "Leave a message."

She heard her own voice, as if from far away, say into the phone, "Warren, I'm lost. I'm lost, and I don't know what to do. Please call me, will you? Please don't let me be alone with these thoughts any longer."

Chapter 31

As Susan sat despairing in her hotel, Warren Lane was knocking on the door of an apartment in Monterey Park, just east of Los Angeles. Yun Zhu was surprised to see a white man when he answered. Noticing the chain was not attached on the inside, Lane pushed his way in and shut the door behind him.

Yun looked at Lane's suit and asked with a mixture of fear and confusion, "You are police?"

"No, I'm not police," Lane said, mocking Yun's grammar. "Why don't you show some hospitality and make me a cup of tea?"

"You want tea?"

"That's what I said."

While Yun filled a teakettle, Lane looked around the apartment. It was a small studio with a futon, a table, and three chairs. A few books and magazines were strewn on the floor, some in English, some in Chinese. On the bare floor beside the futon were a blanket and pillow. The air smelled of stale cigarettes, fish, and fermented beans. The whole apartment had a smothering, claustrophobic atmosphere.

Yun kept his eyes on Lane.

"How many people live here?" Lane asked.

"You police?" Yun asked.

"I told you I'm not the police," Lane said.

"You dress like gentleman."

"How many people live here?" Lane asked again.

"Three," said Yun.

"Your family?"

"No," said Yun. "Family in China. Two other men. Their family also in China."

"Where are they?" Lane asked.

"Work. They work night. I work day."

"At Will Moore's furniture place?" Lane asked.

Yun smiled. "Yes. Mr. Moore send you?"

"No," said Lane.

Yun's smile faded into an anxious look.

Lane pulled his phone from his pocket and pointed it at Yun. "Smile," he said. Yun was startled by the flash.

"Why you take my picture?" Yun asked.

"Mr. Zhu," Lane began.

"Mr. Yun," Yun corrected. "Yun is family name. Zhu is given name."

"Shut up," said Lane. He tapped at the phone a few times before putting it down. "Mr. Yun, do you know who Eduardo Rodriguez is?"

Yun thought for a moment, his eyes still nervously watching Lane. "No," he said. "I don't know him."

"Eduardo Rodriguez is the legitimate owner of the Social Security number you've been using."

All the air went out of Yun. He took his eyes off Lane for the first time as he lifted the kettle with a trembling hand and filled the ceramic teapot.

"He is angry?" Yun asked.

"No, he's dead."

Yun's anxiety and confusion increased. "You police?" he asked again.

"God dammit, I'm not the police, you fucking retard."

"Why you come here?"

"I want you to answer some questions," Lane said.

"Sit," said Yun as he carried two cups to the table. Lane took a seat. Yun filled both cups and sat across from Lane.

"You work for Will Moore," Lane asked. "Is that right?"

"Yes," said Yun. "Mr. Moore is good man. Very fair man. You do good work, he is fair."

"That's sweet," Lane said with mock affection. "What do you do for Mr. Moore?"

"I clean showroom. I clean warehouse. I unload furniture. It's delicate job. You must be careful unpacking antiques."

"Ever drop anything?" Lane asked.

This question startled Yun. "No," he said. "Very careful. Always very careful."

"Sometimes you work nights," Lane said.

"I work days. My roommates work nights at restaurant. We have only two bed."

"But sometimes you work nights, correct?"

"Sometimes," Yun said. "Mr. Moore pays overtime. I work extra hours."

"Sometimes…" said Lane. He paused for a long time and stared at Yun, watching the other man's discomfort grow. "Sometimes you go in at 10:00 p.m. and you work past midnight."

Again, the wind went out of Yun, as if he were struck by a blow. He forced a smile, but the little wrinkles that appeared above his eyebrows betrayed his anxiety. "Sometimes there is extra cleanup," he said.

"It seems to happen about once every three months," Lane said.

Yun picked up a cigarette and a lighter from the table. "When there is overtime, I take it. I save. One day I bring my wife here. My son…" Yun smiled. "My son is six. One day I save enough to bring them here."

Lane pulled the cigarette from Yun's mouth before he could light it. "Don't smoke in here," Lane said. "Show some fucking courtesy."

Lane threw the cigarette on the table and stared at Yun as he explained in a matter-of-fact tone, "You work late at night about once every three months when a truck arrives with a new container from Long Beach. And there's no one else there. It's just you."

Yun smiled and nodded. "I work overtime. I bring my family here. America is wonderful country."

"Good God, you're irritating," Lane said with more than a hint of exasperation. "Why are you unloading containers all by yourself in the middle of the night?"

"Mr. Moore is good man," Yun said, still smiling and nodding. "Give me plenty of work."

Lane took a deep breath to calm himself. He picked up a photo of a young boy from the table. "Is this your son?" he asked.

Yun seized the opportunity to steer the conversation to a more pleasant topic. "Yes. Smart boy. He already understand computer. Good in math too. Someday he come here. He will be computer programmer. He will live in house, not apartment. Will have respect, not be scared."

Lane picked up the cigarette lighter and lit the corner of the photo. He held it by the opposite corner, turning it so the boy's face was toward Yun. As he altered the angle of the photo to increase the flame, he kept his eyes on Yun, whose expression changed from shock to hurt and anger. He wanted to hit Lane, or stab him. But he feared the man.

"You are not worthy of your suit," Yun said bitterly. "You are not gentleman."

"No, I'm not," said Lane. "And you're starting to piss me off. Let me show you something." Lane dropped the photo into the ashtray. He opened the email app on his phone and pulled up a draft. He turned the screen toward Yun and said, "You can read, right?"

"I can read."

"Look."

Yun scanned the email, which was addressed to an officer at Immigration and Customs Enforcement. It included Yun's name, his home address, his work address, his stolen Social Security number, and the photo Lane had taken a few minutes before.

"Do you want your wife to come here?" Lane asked. "Do you want to see your son?"

"Yes," Yun said. "It is all I work for."

"Then I need you to answer some questions. What is in those shipments you unpack?"

Yun hesitated for a long time, looking troubled.

"What's the matter?" Lane asked.

"Mr. Moore is good man."

"Then you'll have nothing bad to report. Tell me what's in the shipments. Drugs?"

"Not drugs," Yun said. "Medicine."

"Medicine?"

"Yes. To help people."

"Moore imports furniture. If he's bringing in medicine, it's not to help people. What kind of medicine?"

"I don't know," Yun said. "Little bottles. The kind you use with needle. Looks like water inside."

"Are they labeled?"

Again, Yun hesitated, and then silently nodded.

"I know you can read. What do the labels say?"

Yun took a breath and turned his eyes up toward the ceiling. "Avastin. Herceptin. Tarceva."

"Do you know what those are?" Lane asked.

Yun looked down at the table. "No."

"Those are cancer medicines. If they were legit, they wouldn't be coming from China in a container full of furniture. They would be refrigerated in transit. Are your containers refrigerated?"

Yun shook his head.

"Where does the medicine go after you unpack it?"

"To another truck."

"Whose truck?"

"I don't know," Yun said, shaking his head again. "I don't know."

Lane stood and extended his hand. "Mr. Zhu. Mr. Yun, whatever your name is, thank you. You've been very helpful."

Yun stood and shook his hand with a look of woe. Then he asked, "Why do you want to know this if you are not police?"

"I'm going to have a talk with Mr. Moore," said Lane.

"You are going to deport me?" Yun asked.

"No," said Lane. "I don't really care about you. I just wanted the information."

As he left, Lane said, "Good luck with your wife and son. The boy sounds bright. If he really knows computers and math, he'll do well here."

"Thank you," said Yun. "The day I see them on this shore, my heart burst with joy."

Yun closed the door behind him. On his way down the hall, Lane pulled the up the email and pressed Send.

Chapter 32

The following morning, Ready tossed fitfully in the late morning sun that streamed onto the bed as Ella lay beside him, peaceful and still. In his dream, he saw Susan falling into bottomless darkness, getting smaller and smaller in the distance as he called to her.

He awoke with a feeling of dread in the pit of his stomach as he remembered that his phone had been off since the previous afternoon. He pulled his phone from the charger and turned it on to find half a dozen missed calls from Susan.

He pulled on his clothes, bent to kiss Ella, and then without saying a word left her sleeping and drove directly to the hotel. He listened to Susan's messages on the way. The tone of her voice in the calls progressed from anguish and despair to exhaustion and numbness. He tried to call her, but she didn't answer.

"I'm coming," he said. "I'm coming, Susan. Hang in there."

She didn't come to the door of her hotel room when he knocked. When he tried her number again, he could hear her phone ringing inside the room. In his growing panic, he convinced a manager to open the door for him, but the room was empty.

In the elevator, he decided to check her house, and if she wasn't there, he would drive the streets around the hotel.

In the lobby, he ran into Omar. "You lookin' for your lady friend?"

"Have you seen her?"

"She walked out about twenty minutes ago," Omar said. "She looked sick."

"Which way did she go?"

"That way," Omar pointed.

Ready jumped into his car and drove slowly down the street, examining every person on the sidewalk. He passed the pharmacy just in time to see Susan walking out, looking pale and weak. He rushed from the car and took her arm to steady her.

"Oh, thank God!" she said.

"Do you need to go to the hospital?" he asked. "You don't look good."

"Just get me away from here," she said wearily. "I don't care where we go. And please don't leave me alone."

He helped her into the car and held her hand as they drove. At the first stoplight, he studied her drained face and the blank exhaustion in her eyes. He removed the bottle from the bag she had carried out of the pharmacy. Sleeping pills.

"You weren't going to kill yourself, were you?" he asked.

"I don't know," she said. "I just wanted to sleep. Maybe for a long time. Maybe forever. I don't know."

The right lane was closed ahead, blocked by police cars and an ambulance. As they passed, they saw a paramedic standing idly with his clipboard and radio while a policeman pulled a sheet over the body of a woman in the crosswalk.

"Oh, God." Susan exclaimed as she turned away. "I didn't need to see that. I'm just a step behind her, Warren. Just one step behind."

"Shhh. Just hold my hand. Just hold on to me, OK?"

He drove her to a red-roofed Mission-style house secluded beneath a rich canopy of palms.

* * *

Inside the house, Susan sat on the end of the guest room bed looking tired and forlorn. She watched Ready return from the bathroom, where she could hear the water running.

"This place is nice," she said. "I wouldn't have guessed it after seeing the beat-up little car you drive."

"It's not my house," Ready said. "I'm just taking care of it."

"Are you going to take a bath?" Susan asked.

"No," said Ready. "You are." He took her hand and helped her up from the bed.

Susan began to tremble as the feelings of dread and anxiety from the previous night returned.

"What's wrong?" he asked.

"It's that dread. It's coming back. Oh, Warren, what am I going to do?"

"Take a deep breath," Ready said.

"I don't mean now," she said wearily. "With my life. What am I going to do at forty, with no husband and no family and no friends? The lawyers keep hinting that Will's in trouble and is going to lose all his money. What if he leaves me with nothing? How will I support myself?"

"Susan, you're smartest person I know. I'm sure you can do something."

"Who's going to give me a job, Warren? I haven't worked in twelve years. I have no skills. I don't even know what people do in offices these days. Who would marry me? Who will love me? Who will be my friend? I have no friends." She sat back down on the bed and started to cry.

"Why are you torturing yourself about tomorrow?" asked Ready. "You have enough to deal with just to get through today."

"Because I need to know. I need a reason to wake up in the morning. I can't open my eyes on another day like today. I just can't. I have to know there's something out there for me. Some reason for being."

"There is no knowing, Susan. There's only faith. You just proceed as if the world will be OK. You live your life like you'll still be here tomorrow. Make plans like you'll get a chance to fulfill them.

Those are acts of faith, because no one really knows whether they'll be here tomorrow. No one really knows anything."

Susan shook her head. "I can't live like that, Warren. I have to know. I have to know that something will be there for me."

As he had at their first meeting in the coffee shop, Ready listened with surprise to the words her desperation drew from his mouth.

"Then you have to make that happen. Make the life you want. You're not that woman under the sheet at the side of the road. Her life is over. Yours isn't. The sun is still shining, and the sky is still blue, and every day from this day forward is a gift that was given to you that she didn't get. So make yourself worthy of it.

"There are people who will be important to you five or ten years from now who you haven't even met yet. Some of them haven't even been born yet. You don't know, Susan. So please don't give up. You just have to go forward and trust."

Ready's words quieted her and she sat still as he wiped the tears from her face with the bottom of his shirt. He took her hand and led her into the bathroom where the mirrors were coated with steam.

"I feel a little woozy," Susan said. "I'm so run down."

"You're tense, too. Do you know that? A bath will help you relax."

Susan stared blankly at the floor as Ready quietly undressed her.

After a minute, she said, "Warren? Why didn't you answer my calls?"

"My phone was off."

"Then how did you know to look for me?"

"I had a dream about you," he said, as he removed her bra. "You were falling. Just falling into bottomless darkness."

She stood before him naked, feeling neither arousal nor shame, for grief had stripped her of all her pride. "I was, Warren. I was."

She thought about his words and accepted that he was right. There was no knowing. She closed her eyes and said to herself: *I give up. I give up. I don't know where I'm going, and I don't know what my life will be. Whatever happens, happens, and I'll make the best of it.*

With this quiet surrender, her anxiety and dread began to melt away. When she opened her eyes again and looked at Ready, she saw in his face the empathy of a fellow sufferer. Why had she met him? Where had all her suffering led her but to this moment? The aching in her heart gave way to a flood of gratitude as she received from him the simple kindness her former pride would not have permitted her to accept. Ready helped her into the water, and she received her baptism.

"I'll be in the other room," Ready said. "Let me know if you need anything."

She lowered her head in gratitude and let go of everything. And this time, when she cried, the hurt flowed out, and she at last found some release.

* * *

Forty minutes later, she left the bathroom in a white terry robe. The steam of the bath had restored the color to her cheeks. The tension and fear had left her body, and she moved with serenity and grace.

Ready lay on the bed watching *Planes, Trains and Automobiles* with the sound turned down low. "You look so much better," he said with relief.

Susan lay down beside him and put her head on his chest. The moisture from her wet, dark hair soaked through his shirt.

"Warren, thank you for being here," she said. "Thank you for what you said."

"You're welcome."

"I'm sorry if I scared you."

She looked at the TV, where John Candy and Steve Martin were driving down the wrong side of the highway. The driver of another car was shouting at them, trying to warn them they were going the wrong way.

"He says we're going the wrong way," said Steve Martin's character.

"Oh, he's drunk," said John Candy. "How would he know where we're going?"

"Do you want me to turn this off?" Ready asked.

"No," she said. "It's nice to see something light for a change. The past few days have been so dark and heavy."

She took four long breaths and was asleep. Ready followed soon after.

* * *

Ready awoke an hour before sunset and searched the kitchen for something to drink, but found no alcohol anywhere. His phone showed a single text from Ella: "Where did you go?? Will's here. Stay away." Ready ate some toast with butter, then went outside and sat in a wicker chair and watched the birds.

He thought about going to get some beer, but when he turned and looked in the window, he saw that Susan was sitting up and looking around. When she saw him, she relaxed and put her head back on the pillow.

Better not leave her, he thought.

He sat for another half hour listening to the breeze and watching little lizards scurry along the ground. *How do people just sit around like this without a drink?* he wondered.

He returned to the bedroom just as the sun disappeared into the Pacific. Susan's robe was on the floor beside the bed and she lay on her side with the sheet pulled up to her shoulder. Ready climbed in beside her and turned on his side to face her. He pushed her hair away from her cheek, and then traced the line of her neck and shoulder and ran his fingers down the length of her arm. When he looked up, she was watching him.

"How long have you been awake?" he asked.

"Since you came in."

Ready pushed the sheet down to her waist and ran his hand slowly along her side. Susan turned onto her back, pushed the sheet down to her thighs and stretched. Her full, soft body was something new to him, and deeply welcoming. He had never been with a woman older than himself. He kissed her breasts, drew his fingers slowly across her belly, and stroked the insides of her thighs.

She watched him calmly as he explored her body. She knew his hand found blemishes on her skin and softness in flesh that had once been firm. In the past, she would have moved away instinctively from a man's touch as it approached her imperfections. Or she would have guided his hand to some other area that had passed her own strict inspection during the daily inventory of her body.

But now, she accepted from him the approval and admiration she denied herself, as she began to understand what he had said to her on the day of their hike: *all joy begins with yes.*

After they made love, she fell into a deep and dreamless sleep.

Chapter 33

Susan and Ready awoke early the next morning, well rested from their long hours in bed. Neither made a move to get up.

"Warren, do you remember before the hike, when you said, *All joy begins with yes?* Did you make that up?"

"I don't know. Maybe. I had a revelation on the boat one night."

Susan turned to face him, propping herself on one elbow.

Ready continued: "Have you ever taken acid?"

"No."

"When you trip, there's a peak where you might be hallucinating, and then there's this long period of coming down that can last for several hours. You don't really hallucinate then, but you see patterns, and your thoughts are kind of weird.

"Anyway, I was coming down from a trip a few weeks ago, and I was restless. The sky was clear and the moon was bright, and the breeze was light, so I took the boat out. I went out against the wind, tacking. You know, zigzagging. Then I turned around and opened the sails and was on a run back toward shore. When you're on a run, going with the wind, it's very quiet. Even though you're moving, the air feels almost still around you. I looked behind me, and I saw the smooth silver trail the boat had cut through the sea. Then I looked in front of me, and I saw the same trail open out ahead of me. It was like I was seeing the road I was about to travel.

"I took the sails in, and the path in front of me disappeared. I let them out again, the boat picked up speed, and the path came back. And I had this revelation. Open your sails to the wind, and your path will open up before you. In life that means saying yes. There's always some force pushing you toward destiny. You just have to be open and accept it and not try to control it."

"I'm starting to understand that now," Susan said.

"I've been trying to live my life that way for the past few weeks. Saying yes to things I would normally avoid. It's been interesting."

"What kinds of things have you said yes to?"

"Well, like...to you." Ready was thinking of the morning in the coffee shop, when Susan mistook him for Warren Lane and he agreed to help her. But Susan interpreted it differently. In her mind, he had said yes to being her lover, if only for a night.

"Warren," she said.

"Hmm?"

"Will you take me back to the hotel? I want to change my clothes."

"Sure."

"Are you hungry?" Susan asked.

"A little."

"I'll make you some breakfast."

She kissed him and got up from the bed.

"You just going to walk around naked?" Ready asked.

She looked over her shoulder at him with a little smile as she walked into the kitchen. On this particular morning, she felt beautiful and free in a way she hadn't ever before. They took their time over breakfast, and an hour and a half later, they drove to the hotel.

Chapter 34

As Ready and Susan were on their way the hotel, Will stood alone in the kitchen of the house in Goleta, looking gloomy. He had arrived in a good mood the night before, but was unhappy and irritable by the time he went to bed. For the first time in his relationship with Ella, he could not perform. Ella did nothing to encourage him. When he started snoring, she went downstairs and slept on the couch.

The news article that had soured his mood just before bed was still weighing on his mind when his phone rang.

"Will?" It was the manager of his LA warehouse. "We just got a visit from an immigration officer. They have Yun in custody."

"What?" Will exclaimed. His throat and chest tightened.

"They want to go through our employee records. He's illegal. They're looking for more."

"We don't have any other illegals," Will said.

"How do you know that?"

"Because I know," Will said.

"Wait, did you know Yun was illegal?"

Ignoring the question, Will asked, "Did you talk to Yun?"

"No. But he was looking very anxious yesterday. He told one of the other employees that a man came to his apartment the night before and threatened him."

"Fuck!" Will exclaimed.

"Any idea what that's about?"

"I think I might know who he's talking about. Listen," said Will, "don't give anything to immigration. The lawyers will handle this. We have to get Yun out of there. I'll call you back."

Ella entered the kitchen just as Will hung up.

"What's wrong?" she asked. "You look sick. You look like you did that day at the pool in Miami."

Will just shook his head and said, "Fuck."

"Are you OK?" Ella asked.

"I'm going to take a shower," he said, letting out a long breath. "Will you put on some coffee?"

"Sure."

Fifteen minutes later, while drinking coffee and eating a slice of toast, Ella sat staring at Will's phone, which lay facedown on the counter. Her boredom and curiosity got the better of her, and she didn't notice that the shower had stopped. When she picked up the phone and entered his passcode, the screen displayed the name of the person who had just called. She touched the back arrow at the bottom of the phone, and the browser opened to show the *LA Times* article that had ruined Will's mood the night before.

The headline said: *Bogus Meds Traced To LA, Two Arrested in Chicago.* The story began:

Federal investigators announced today the arrest of two men in Chicago on charges of distributing counterfeit cancer drugs. A source close to the investigation says the drugs arrived in Chicago on a train from Los Angeles.

Experts are trying to determine whether the vials contained any of the drugs' active ingredients. One source noted that the rail container was not refrigerated, and that heat would have damaged even legitimate doses of the medicine.

Ella looked up to find Will standing in front of her, his face hard with anger.

"Oops!" she said.

Will grabbed her by the throat and pinned her against the wall. "Are you spying on me?" he demanded. "Are you giving information to that private eye?"

Ella shook her head with the little bit of movement she could manage against his grip. He tightened his fingers around her throat, and her eyes began to water and bulge.

"Do not fuck with me," Will threatened. "Don't fuck with me, or my phone, or any of my stuff. Do not get into my business. Do you understand?"

She nodded.

He let her go and walked across the kitchen and poured himself a cup of coffee. As he took a sip, an apple hit the cup, splashing hot coffee over his face and shirt. The next apple hit him in the head.

"Don't you *ever* come near me again, you monster! I hate you!" Another apple hit his head. "I hate you!" Ella screamed hoarsely.

Will charged her, but with her agility and speed, she easily avoided him. She ran from the house, and shouted "Monster!" one last time as she fled the yard.

Chapter 35

Will returned to the kitchen and dumped the coffee into the sink. He filled the mug with Scotch and ice, and then sat on the living room couch and stared out the window toward Josie's house. What had brought him to the point of attacking a woman half his size?

He thought back to the night in Shanghai almost two years earlier when the man named Lee, the one among the dinner guests whose English was nearly fluent, had asked him so many questions about his business. It wasn't until the day after the dinner that he realized Lee had been interviewing him.

"What are the red flags that will automatically cause a container to be inspected? How much do the X-rays reveal? What do the agents look for when acting on their own judgment? Do you know the agents personally? If they know you and you've been doing business through the same port for years, are your containers less likely to be inspected?"

He wasn't surprised when a messenger invited him to drop by Lee's office. The office was in the back of a small warehouse. In the front was a clean, state-of-the-art chemical lab. The two men and one woman who worked in the lab greeted him as if they had been expecting him.

Lee offered Will fifty thousand dollars up front for "including some items" in his next shipment to Long Beach. He would receive another two hundred thousand when the items were delivered to a warehouse in Los Angeles. It had been two months since Will's accountant had lectured him about his extravagance. The lecture did nothing to change Will's spending, but he remembered the words each time he travelled, and they annoyed him. Will asked only how much the items weighed, how much space they occupied, and what they might look like when X-rayed.

Lee took him to the front of the lab and showed him a small paper box, about an inch and a half high, printed in English. He withdrew from the box a glass vial with a metal ring around the top.

"A few hundred of these," Lee said. "Not much room. Not much weight. The metal rings might look funny on X-ray. You decide how to pack them. That is your expertise."

The first shipment went well, providing Will an instant quarter million dollars of tax-free cash. In the second shipment, he had packed the vials into two giant urns. The urns' position in the center of the container and their lead glaze would help obscure their contents from X-rays, if the container happened to be stopped.

But Will had anticipated the wrong risk. Rough seas, hot weather and poor packing caused some of the vials in one urn to break. Yun called him from the loading dock to tell him what happened. While the container broiled in the sun, the leaked medicine had begun to putrefy. There was a noticeable odor.

The urn was supposed to go to the museum, and Will insisted it be rinsed before being delivered. Bleach would remove the smell. He told Yun to wait until he arrived. While tipping the urn to empty the rinse water, he and Yun let it drop and shatter. In a panic, they packed the pieces back into the crate. Yun, terrified of his sweating angry boss, was grateful for not being fired.

That was Will's first warning to get out of the business, but a friendly talk with Lee put him back in good spirits. Why *not* earn an extra $250,000 for shipments he was making anyway? Why not make it $300,000?

The second warning came when he was in Miami and his container got stuck in customs. Sitting alone on the couch of his hotel room after his visit to the hospital, he managed to calm himself from the day's shock and think through the situation rationally. He composed in his mind the words he'd say to Lee to end their little arrangement. But then Ella returned unexpectedly and distracted him from his thoughts. He paid her hotel bill and on the flight home, as he considered again the value of ready cash, he reformulated his conversation with Lee. He would ask for more money, citing the increased risk.

Ten days later, during an unscheduled meeting in Lee's office in Shanghai, Lee balked at Will's request. He wasn't authorized to pay what Will was asking.

"Authorized by whom?" Will asked.

"By Hu. Hu is in charge."

"Let me talk to him," Will said.

Lee shook his head. "You don't want to talk to him. You know what Hu means in Chinese? It means tiger. He is a good businessman, and he is fair if you serve him well, but your request will make him angry. You are getting $300,000, and you should be grateful."

Will sat quietly for several minutes before Lee finally asked, with a look of worry, "You have doubts?"

"I don't think I want to be in this business anymore," Will said slowly.

"I won't tell Hu that," Lee said.

"No, you tell him. Go ahead and tell him. I'm done."

Will stood to leave, but Lee stepped in front of him. "I'll tell Hu nothing. Listen, you go along while you're still on good terms. Or he'll take over, and you'll have no say in the matter."

"Tell him I'm done," said Will. He shoved Lee out of the way and left.

He was relieved when he quit, and thought it was all over. But now, as he sipped Scotch on the gilded couch in his house full of treasures, he realized the reckoning was approaching from all sides.

The story of Ben Schwartz's wife had pricked his conscience, suffusing him with a vague, persistent anxiety. The federal investigators would eventually find their way to him now that Yun was in custody. He assumed his wife already knew of Ella from Warren Lane.

Ella was the one remaining bright spot in his life, and he had just strangled her. He let out a loud groan as he pressed the icy mug of Scotch to his forehead. "Oh, God. What the hell am I doing?"

He remembered the fake passport in his desk at work. Most of his smuggling money was in the account in Hong Kong. He would need a day or two to settle matters at work, and then he would fly to Asia.

The thought of abandoning Susan, whom he had already betrayed, and leaving her to clean up this mess on her own filled him with shame. But he knew she wouldn't go with him once Warren Lane and the feds showed her who he had become. He was already starting to think of her as part of his past.

Before he left the house, he paid off Ella's credit cards. This was an act of contrition, the one wrong he still had the power to set right.

Chapter 36

Ready was watching TV in Susan's room at the Canary while Susan showered. When his phone rang, he muted the television and said, "Hello?"

"Warren?" Ella was crying and hyperventilating.

"What's wrong?"

"Will tried to strangle me. He slammed me against the wall and strangled me."

"What the fuck?" Ready said. "Take a breath. Where are you?"

"Driving. State Street, near Figueroa. Where are you?"

"At the Canary. About a block from where you are."

"Which room?" Ella asked.

"302."

"I'll be there in two minutes."

"Wait! No!"

But she had already hung up. Ready heard the shower turn off. He burst into the bathroom and said, "Susan, you have to leave."

"What? Why?" she asked, as she reached for a towel.

"Please don't ask, just get out."

"What's the matter with you?"

Ready returned to the bed and pulled a skirt and blouse from Susan's bag and threw them at her in the bathroom. "Put these on and get out," Ready said.

"What's gotten into you? I need a bra and underwear."

"You can come back later and get those," Ready said.

Still dripping, Susan stepped into the skirt and put her arms through the sleeves of the blouse. Ready opened the door to the hallway and looked toward the elevators. Then he returned to the room and put Susan's bag and loose clothing into the closet.

171

Susan came out of the bathroom to find him carrying a pair of her shoes. "What are you doing with those?"

"Putting them in the closet."

"Give them to me," she said. "I'll wear them. What's going on Warren? Are you married?"

"No," said Ready, clearly in distress. "There's someone coming I don't want you to see."

"You don't want me to see them," Susan asked, "or you don't want them to see me?"

"Both."

Susan studied him for a second with a curious look, then said, "OK, Warren. I'll go. Will you tell me what this is about?"

"Later, I promise," Ready said.

With her hair dripping and wet spots all over her clothes, Susan threw her arms around his neck and gave him a long kiss on the mouth. Her back was to the door, and as they parted, Ready opened his eyes to see Ella standing just outside. Her mouth was expressionless and her eyes were filled with hurt. The sight of her took all the wind out of him, and the same feelings of disappointment and betrayal that shot through her heart shot through his.

Ella turned and walked away. Susan never realized anyone was behind her. When she opened her eyes and saw the pained expression on Ready's face, she said, "What's wrong? What is it?"

Ready couldn't speak.

Chapter 37

Will Moore awoke alone in his own bed at nine o'clock the next morning. His cell phone was ringing but he didn't recognize the number.

"Hello?" he said.

"Good morning, Mr. Moore," came the taunting voice from the other end.

"Who is this?" Will asked irritably.

"Warren Lane."

"What the hell do you want?"

"Well, first of all, I'd like to congratulate your wife on that little stunt she pulled the other day. No one's ever gotten me quite like that."

"What are you talking about?"

"Never mind. Look, Will, I've been doing a little investigation into your business and I've uncovered some very interesting things. Perhaps we should meet to discuss how to handle this matter."

"Fuck off," Will said, and ended the call.

Ten minutes later, he was in the kitchen when the front door opened. He walked out to see who was there.

"I was surprised to see your car out front," Susan said. "I thought you'd be at work by now. I just came to get a few things."

Will stood looking at her, and for the first time since that day in the bookstore thirteen years ago, he didn't know what to say. Finally, he said, "You want some coffee? Come into the kitchen."

"I don't want coffee," she said as she followed him into the kitchen. "I'm going to get my own apartment, Will. I can't be with you anymore, and you know why."

Will looked at her thoughtfully for a long moment and then said with genuine regret, "I'm sorry, Susan."

"You should be," she said. She was calm and fully in possession of herself. "How could you betray me like that? Do you know how much it hurts to lose faith in the person you trusted above all others? Do you know how much it hurts to find no love in your heart for the one you wanted to love forever? It's the bitterest thing a person can feel."

Will sat on a stool at the kitchen island and hung his head and let his shoulders slump.

"I have a lawyer," Susan said. "And we have evidence. I know this isn't a one-time thing. I know what you've been doing."

Will looked at her sorrowfully and said, "I won't fight you, Susan. I won't make you suffer anymore. Tell me what you want, and it's yours."

Susan felt a touch of pity for the man. He let out a long slow breath and then asked in a weary voice, "Who is he?"

"Who is who?" But she knew what he was asking.

"Who are you sleeping with?" he asked. "The manager at the hotel told me about your visitor."

She didn't want to tell him it was the detective she had hired to investigate him. That would be an unnecessary provocation. So she said, "Just someone I met by chance. He's a good man." Then, thinking back to the day Ready found her in front of the pharmacy, she added, "Some angel must have thrown him in my path."

"Do you love him?" Will asked, still looking down toward the floor.

"Very much," Susan said.

Will nodded. "You deserve it, Susan," he said. "You deserve someone who will make you happy. What's his name?"

"Warren," she replied. "Warren Lane."

At the mention of this name, Will's hands began to tremble, and Susan instinctively stepped away from him. Will felt his control slipping away, as it had the day before when he attacked Ella. In a trembling voice, he said to her, "Get out of here, Susan. I'm going to hurt you. Run, Susan, run!" he begged.

She did as he asked, and was gone.

For several minutes after she left, Will tried to steady his breathing. He wouldn't allow himself to move until he was certain she was gone. When he finally got up, he filled a glass with Scotch and ice, and his phone rang again. This time it was his mother.

"What?" said Will irritably.

"What yourself!" his mother snapped. "Don't answer the phone like that."

"Sorry, ma. I'm a little on edge this morning." He took a sip of Scotch.

"Sounds like it," his mother said. "I hear ice tinkling. You're not drinking, are you?"

"I'm afraid it's that kind of day," said Will.

"Well, have one for me while you're at it. I'm having that kind of day too. You know what's wrong with my day, son? I don't have my pills."

"Relax," Will said. "I'll drop them by before lunch."

"Well aren't we cranky this morning?" his mother replied. "When you finish that drink, go ahead and pour yourself another. I don't want you bringing that attitude into *my* retirement home."

"All right, ma."

She hung up, and as Will poured himself a second drink, his phone rang again.

"Hi, Will," said Ella.

Will took a deep breath. "What do *you* want?" he asked.

"I just wanted to say I'm sorry for what I did yesterday."

"You don't have to apologize," Will said. "If anyone should apologize, it's me."

"I know you're under a lot of stress, Will. I can see it. Maybe you need to blow off a little steam."

"I don't know if today's the day for that."

"I'm really horny," Ella said. "I keep running the washing machine on spin cycle just so I can rub myself against the corner of it."

"It's that bad?" Will asked. The image of her pressing against the vibrating machine aroused him.

"It's that bad," Ella said.

The Scotch was beginning to do its job, and a sense of warm wellbeing washed over him. In his mind, he saw her naked again on that balcony in Miami, with the warm sea stretched out behind her. He pictured her lithe body moving beneath him, the sweat on her forehead, the flush in her cheeks, the clear blue eyes looking up at him.

"You know what you are?" Will said.

"What?"

"You are my sunshine."

"That's sweet, Will. How soon can you get here?"

"Half an hour. I have to stop and pick up a prescription."

"I'll be waiting."

She hung up. Will finished his Scotch and got into his car.

Chapter 38

As Will was on his way to Ella's house, Ready stood at a gas pump, filling his tank with one hand and holding his phone to his ear with the other. "Come on, Ella. Answer. Please answer!"

When her voicemail picked up, he said, "Ella, I'm sorry! Please call me. Please! I have to see you, Ella. I love you, and I'm sorry!"

The gas nozzle clicked. Ready laid his phone on the roof of the car as he put the nozzle back into its holder. He bought a six-pack in the mini-mart and opened a beer as he drove toward Ella's house. As he accelerated onto the Pacific Coast Highway, his phone slid off the back of the car and was crushed beneath the wheel of the truck behind him.

Will arrived at Ella's house about a minute before Ready did. The drive gave Will time to think about his wife and Warren Lane, and once again his anger began to rise. Josie was standing on Ella's doorstep when Will got out of the car. Before going up the walk, he took a moment to calm himself so he wouldn't frighten her.

"Hello, little girl," he said in the politest tone he could muster. "What have you got there?"

She showed him the little flowers she had picked. "Flowers for Miss Ella," she said. "And her boyfriend."

Ready watched the two of them talk from his little blue Toyota as he cruised slowly past the house. "Fuck!" he exclaimed. "Go away, you bastard!"

"What boyfriend?" Will asked.

"The one who takes her upstairs and makes her scream 'Oh God! Oh God! Oh God!'" said Josie.

Ready drove away.

"Get out of my way, you little shit," said Will. He pushed her aside and burst through the door. "Ella!" he screamed.

Ella was standing next to the liquor tray in the living room. She knew this would be their final confrontation, and she couldn't suppress a little smile at seeing Will so upset.

"Get ahold of yourself, Will. You're going to have a heart attack."

Will's phone rang. The screen said "Mother." He rejected the call.

"Who are you fucking in *my* house?" he demanded hotly.

"You want a drink Will? You really need to calm down." She poured a glass of Scotch and walked toward him with the glass in one hand and the bottle in the other.

Just as she reached him, she leapt with a dancer's strength and grace and kicked him in the crotch with all her might. She let out a little laugh as he crumpled to the floor.

"What was it you wanted to know, Will?" she asked in a gentle, teasing tone. "Who am I fucking? Was that the question?" She took a sip of Scotch, then stood on the toes of her left foot and twirled like a ballerina. Unable to draw a breath, Will looked up at her with a red face and watery eyes.

"What's the matter?" Ella asked, mocking a look of concern. "Is little Willie sad?"

She walked in a circle around him, smiling her girlish smile. His phone rang again. Ella picked it up from the rug and looked at the screen.

"It's your mommy, Will. Why don't you talk to her? Maybe she can make you feel better." She swiped to accept the call, then handed him the phone.

Holding it to his ear, all Will could do for several seconds was gasp in pain. Finally, he grunted, "Hello?"

"Good God, William!" barked his mother. "Don't answer the phone while you're having sex! This is your mother, for Christ's sake! Have some decency. Do you have my medicine?"

Will grunted a few more times before he was able to gasp out the word, "Yeah."

"Well, when are you going to bring it to me?" she demanded. "It sounds like you're busy. You tell that sweet wife of yours I say hello. Go on. Tell her right now. Is she enjoying herself, William? You can tell if you look at her face."

She paused for a moment then added, "You finish up your business, and take your time about it. A woman doesn't like to be rushed. And when you're done, you get over here with my medicine. I feel like shit."

She hung up.

"Do you really want to know who I'm fucking?" Ella asked, hovering lightly behind him. "It's a friend of yours, Will."

"What friend?" Will grunted, still doubled over on the floor.

She circled back in front of him. "Your best friend."

"I don't have a best friend," Will said looking up at her.

"Oh?" said Ella, feigning sadness. "He told me he was your best friend, and it made me come."

"Who is it?" Will asked in a tone of pained desperation.

"Warren Laaaaaaane," Ella said, stretching out the name for effect.

Will's face went from red to purple, and his whole body began to shake.

"Oh, my!" said Ella with delight. "That one hit the mark!"

She poured the bottle of Scotch onto the rug and threw a match on it. She grabbed her keys from the table by the front door, and as the puddle of flame began to lick the sofa, she said, "Get out while you can, Will. Good bye!"

She blew a kiss behind her as she left the house, and then drove off into the hills.

Ready was several minutes ahead of her on the same road. While Ella was still ascending the mountain with her music at full volume, Ready hiked up to his rock, carrying his six-pack with him. For a long time he sat looking out over the city.

A young man and a young woman came by with a pack of children. They all wore matching T-shirts that said Camp Sunshine. The children picked up stones and drew in the dirt with sticks as the counselors unpacked their snacks. Wary of Ready and his beer bottles, the young woman steered the kids away from him.

Ready paid them no attention and didn't notice when they left. But as he finished his sixth beer, the blaring music from a car descending the road below seemed to awaken him, and he realized he had been staring for some time at a stream of dark grey smoke rising from the northern edge of Goleta. He did some calculations in his head and concluded, "That's Ella's neighborhood."

That was excuse enough to drive back into town. If Ella wasn't home, he'd buy more beer.

Chapter 39

By the time Will made it to his feet, the couch was on fire. "Fuck it!" he said. "I'll be out of the country tonight. Fuck this place. Fuck Goleta. Fuck Santa Barbara. Fuck California!" He opened the freezer and packed some ice into a plastic bag, then went out the back door as the kitchen filled with smoke.

He drove straight to his mother's retirement home, where Lucille watched him walk in gingerly, holding the bag of ice against his crotch.

"What's the matter?" his mother asked. "Have the girls been teasing you?"

"Some little prick is trying to ruin my life," Will said.

"William, I've known since you were in high school exactly which little prick was going to ruin your life. Don't try to blame your problems on other people. You're too indulgent with yourself, and you don't have enough consideration for others. You wouldn't have been able to get away with half the things you've done if it weren't for your money. Now where's my medicine?"

Will handed her the bottle of pills. When she struggled to open it, he pulled the cap off for her.

"Thank you," said Lucille. "Now what kind of trouble have you gotten yourself into this time?"

"Some private investigator is after me," Will said. "Some asshole named Warren Lane."

"Warren Lane," Lucille repeated fondly. "He's a looker, that one."

"You know him?" Will asked, startled.

"Oh, yes," she said. "He paid me quite a visit one day. And boy, has that fella got a cock on him!"

"What?" Will exclaimed.

"I tell you, that fella has a woody that just won't quit."

"What are you talking about? What woody? How would you know if he had a woody?"

"Well, he practically forced it on me," Lucille said. There was a hint of pride in her tone.

The thought of his mother touching the genitals of that vain, arrogant, skinny little beak-faced man filled Will with disgust, and his face flushed a deep shade of crimson.

"I did my best to oblige him," Lucille continued. "At my age, I don't get many chances. Of course, in the end he just ran off like they all do. But at least I've got the memory. Just hearing that name brings a smile to my face."

The crimson spread to Will's scalp and neck, and he began to shake with rage.

"I'll kill that motherfucker!" he screamed as he hobbled out of the room. All the way down the hall, Lucille heard him shouting, "I'll kill him! I will kill him!"

Chapter 40

Ready picked up another six-pack on his way into town, and was halfway through the first bottle when he reached Ella's street, which was lined with fire trucks. A fireman waved at him, and Ready rolled down his window.

"Street's closed," the fireman said.

"I live here," Ready replied.

The fireman looked down the street, then back at Ready. "OK. Just take it slow. There are a lot of people around, and no one's looking for cars. So watch out. And get rid of that beer."

"Yes, sir," Ready said, putting the beer bottle into the cup holder.

He drove slowly down the street, and to his horror, saw that it was Ella's house that had burned. Abandoning his car between the fire trucks, he ran up the walk and tried to enter the dripping, smoldering house. Two firemen pulled him back.

"You can't go in there. What's wrong with you?"

"Was anyone in the house when it burned?" Ready asked urgently.

"We can't tell yet," said one of the firemen. "We don't think so, but we haven't searched everywhere."

Seeing Josie standing with her mother in front of the house next door, Ready broke free of the firemen's grasp and ran to her.

"Did you see Miss Ella? Do you know if she got out?"

Josie looked up at him with her habitual serious expression. "I don't know, mister." She handed him the flowers she had picked. Ready turned and walked back to his car, which was still idling in the middle of the street.

"Where is she?" he said to no one in particular.

"Do you know that man?" Josie's mother asked.

The little girl turned her dark eyes up to her mother and said, "That's the man who drinks too much and sleeps in his car. Miss Ella loves him."

Chapter 41

Downtown, still hobbling with the ice pack pressed between his legs, Will Moore burst through the double glass doors of Lane Investigation. Grunting like a wounded bull, he headed straight for the glass-walled conference room where Lane sat talking with a man in a suit.

Maxine leapt from her desk and tried to intercept him. "Sir," she said with fear in her voice. "Sir, you can't go in there!"

Will pushed her to the floor with his right hand and walked into the meeting room. At the sight of his angry hobble and dripping ice pack, Warren Lane demanded in a tone of contempt, "What the fuck do *you* want?"

"You fucked my wife, you fucked my girlfriend, and you fucked my mother!" Will shouted.

"Oh my God, he's gone insane!" said Lane, with a mocking grin.

Will raised a pistol with his right hand and pointed it across the table toward Lane, whose face melted into an expression of abject terror. Before Lane could say a word, Will put a bullet through his heart. Then he turned and hobbled out, leaving Maxine and the other man frozen in shock.

Chapter 42

After hours of driving through the hills above the city, alternately laughing and crying, a great hunger came over Ella as she returned to the streets of Santa Barbara. She thought of Ready.

Warren, I want you back. Tell me anything! Give me any excuse for kissing that woman and I'll take it if it makes sense. I just want you back. I want to put that mess behind me. I want to start over, and I want to do it with you.

When she reached for her phone to call him, it wasn't there. *Shit*, she thought. *I left it in the house.*

She parked in front of a juice bar. At the counter inside, she ordered a mango smoothie. The bar was empty except for the woman behind the counter and an older couple sitting quietly in the corner. Ella turned to the window and watched the cars go by on the street while she waited for her drink.

After the whirr of the blender stopped, a woman's voice on the television behind her said, "A shooting in a downtown office late this morning left one man dead."

Ella felt a cold terror rise within her. She put her hand to her mouth and said, "Oh, why did I egg him on? Why did I taunt that violent, angry man?"

"The victim was identified as Warren Lane, a private investigator," said the voice on the TV.

The world went black as Ella collapsed.

Months later, she recalled the older couple in the juice bar standing over her, the paramedics putting the cuff around her arm to measure her blood pressure, and bits and pieces of the ambulance ride. She remembered leaving the hospital against the doctor's advice, and the pitying old man at the airport who let her borrow his phone.

She remembered her hysterical words to her sister on the other end of the line: "I'll be at JFK at midnight. No, I can't take a cab! I can't!" The other passengers in the terminal stared at the snot and tears that poured from her face. "Please pick me up, Anna! I'm begging you! Please help me! Please!"

Chapter 43

Susan was sitting on her bed in the hotel room, looking at her phone, when the news of Lane's murder appeared on TV.

"A shooting in a downtown office late this morning left one man dead. The victim was identified as Warren Lane, a private detective. Witnesses say local business owner William Moore walked into Lane's office and shot him to death, apparently without provocation."

Susan looked up at the screen and blurted, "Oh, God, Will. What have you done?"

"Police say Lane may have been investigating Moore's personal and business affairs."

The screen showed a photo of Lane, with his slicked-back hair, long nose, and green eyes. The caption beneath the photo said *Warren Lane.*

"That's not Warren Lane," Susan said.

A second later, her phone rang.

"Hello?"

"Susan?" It was her lawyer. "Are you at the Canary?"

"Yes."

"I'm on my way to pick you up. Did you hear the news?"

"Yes, but… that's not Warren."

"When the press finds you, they won't leave you alone. Pack a bag and meet me in front of the hotel in five minutes."

"Where are you taking me?"

"Away. And Susan," he added.

"Yes?"

"We did a little digging into Will's business and all I can say is… this is going to be a mess. A big, big mess."

Susan made no response.

"Susan? Are you still there?"

"I'm here," she said.

"Meet me in front of the hotel."

"I will."

Chapter 44

Twenty minutes after Susan left the Canary, Ready pulled up in front. He had eight beers in him now and was visibly drunk. "You can't park that here, sir. I can park it for you if you'd like," said the valet. Ready ignored him and walked into the hotel with his keys in hand.

He went directly to room 302, but no one answered. He instinctively reached for his phone, but it wasn't there. He remembered leaving it on the roof of the car back at the gas station. "Shit!"

He went to the front desk and asked the attendant if he had seen Susan Moore. "She checked out a little while ago," the man said.

"Any idea where she went?"

"I don't know. A car picked her up outside."

Ready returned to his car and drove to Susan and Will's house. There was a crowd of police cars and news trucks in front of the driveway. Pulling up next to a man with a television camera, Ready asked, "What's going on?"

"A murder."

"Here?" Ready asked in panic.

"No," said the cameraman. "The shooter lives here."

"Will?"

"William Moore," the man said.

"Did he shoot her before he burned the house?" Ready asked in a panic. "Oh God, please don't tell me he did that."

The cameraman looked at the house. "This house isn't burned. And it was a man he shot. A detective named Warren Lane."

"But I'm Warren Lane." Ready was sinking into confusion. "What about Susan? Where is Susan?"

"The wife?"

"Yes," Ready said.

The cameraman shrugged. "No one knows. First one to find her gets the prize."

An hour later, Ready was back at the mission style house, grimly opening the first in a series of bottles that would fuel his long descent into darkness.

Chapter 45

Six weeks after Will murdered Warren Lane and Susan and Ella disappeared from his life, Ready stood in the kitchen of Gary's house, pouring himself a bourbon and soda with unsteady hands. Gary and Rebecca sat at the table behind him. The counters were covered with empty beer and wine bottles. The party guests had left.

"Do you really need another drink, Mark?" Rebecca asked.

"Why not?" Gary said. "He's so fuckin' tanked, one more isn't going to make a difference."

"You're just as drunk as he is," Rebecca said.

"You stickin' up for your little pretty boy?" Gary asked. "Hey, Mark. First time Rebecca saw you, she said she wanted to fuck you."

"I did not," Rebecca protested. "I would never say something like that."

"You thought it," Gary said. "Remember?" he said to Ready. "You were in your underwear, and she couldn't stop looking at you. You know what she said? She said she wanted to mother you."

"You're being rude," Ready said. "I'm as drunk as you are and even I think you're being rude."

"So, now it's you two," said Gary, pointing back and forth between Ready and Rebecca, "you two against me, huh?"

"It's not anyone against anyone," Rebecca said. "I think you should go to bed."

Gary turned his attention back to Ready and said, "You know what your problem is, Mark? You're a loser. Seriously. You're twenty-eight years old, and you're a house sitter. A boat sitter. You wash a rich guy's cars and clean his yard. You know, when I was twenty-eight, I was building my second software company. I was four years from retirement. Where are you gonna be in four years?"

"Dead," said Ready.

"That's right, because you're a loser. And you drink like...like you're *trying* to kill yourself. Matter of fact..." Gary got up from the table with an effort that required two attempts. "...matter of fact, here."

He took Ready's drink and dumped it in the sink. Then he put the glass back in Ready's hand and filled it to the top with straight bourbon.

"There you go. Drink that. Maybe that'll finish you off."

Ready drank two ounces of it before Rebecca could take the glass from him.

"Gary, you're being an ass. You're an awful drunk," she said.

"That's why I don't do it all the time," Gary said. "Maybe if I was good at it like Mark here, I'd get drunk more often." Then turning back to Ready, he said, "You used to be a good worker. You used to take care of things. Now everywhere I go, I find your puke. What the hell happened to you? Have you been sober for even a minute since we came back?"

Ready shook his head.

"No?" Gary asked. "Is that a no? Well, at least you're honest. Now *I'm* going to be honest. I don't want you around anymore. You're worthless. You're a sad, moping drunk, and you don't clean anything, and I can't rely on you for anything. It's time for you to move on."

"OK," Ready said.

"Why don't you leave now? Go back to the boat and pack up all your shit. I want you out by morning."

"Oh, Gary, he can't drive," Rebecca said. "Look at him."

"Maybe he'll get lucky and go over a cliff," Gary said. "No point in him going on like this."

Ready stared at him for a second through bleary eyes, then said, "Bye, Gary." He fished his keys from his pocket and added, "Bye, Rebecca."

"Mark, you can't drive!" Rebecca insisted. She tried to follow him from the house, but Gary held her back as Ready went through the front door.

After several attempts, Ready managed to get his key into the ignition. A few seconds later, he smashed into a tree at the end of the driveway. At the sound of the crash, Rebecca ran to the car, with Gary staggering behind her. She opened the driver side door. The air bag was stained with blood from Ready's nose. Ready looked dazed and sick.

"Are you OK, Mark?" Rebecca asked. "Are you all right?"

Gary staggered up behind her and said, "Christ, look what you did to my tree."

Rebecca spun around and slapped him.

"What's that for?" Gary asked.

She pushed him to the ground. As Gary tried without success to stand up, Rebecca helped Ready from the car.

"You're staying here tonight. You're not driving. Understand?" Ready nodded.

* * *

Ready slept until 2:00 p.m. the next day. Rebecca was at his bedside with a damp washcloth and a bowl of water when he awoke.

"You threw up while you were falling asleep," she said.

Ready looked at her with bloodshot eyes.

"You need help, Mark. I don't know what made you take this turn. Gary said you didn't used to be this bad."

Ready closed his eyes.

"You're going to die, Mark. Do you understand that? You're going to die if you don't get some help."

She waited for a response, but he gave none.

"Do you want help, Mark? Have you had enough?"

He opened his eyes again.

"Gary and I will pay for it. We'll send you to rehab. Will you go?"

Ready continued to look at her, but made no response.

"Mark, I'm asking you: Do you want to live, or do you want to die?"

Ready considered the question in silence for a long time. Finally, he said, "I want to live."

"Then you have to go to rehab. You have to. I can take you now. I've been on the phone all morning. I found a place that will take you today. Please, Mark!"

"OK."

It was three more hours before he was able to make it out of bed. Rebecca helped him into the kitchen, where coffee and toast were waiting.

Gary came in as Ready was finishing his coffee. "Hey!" he shouted in a jovial tone that insulted the quiet of the house. "There's the champ! Man, I have no idea how you can drink like that every day. I have the worst hangover ever. Shit!"

Gary paused a moment, then said, "Hey, uh...Rebecca said I was really mean to you last night. I don't know what I said. But I'm sorry."

"It's OK," Ready said.

"Do you remember anything I said?" Gary asked.

"No. Except you fired me."

"Oh, well, nothing I said last night holds. We're going to get you to rehab, and if there's anything you need while you're in there or after you get out, you just ask."

"Thanks, Gary."

"Are you ready to go?" Rebecca asked.

"I'm ready," Ready said.

"OK. Gary, I'll see you tomorrow?" Rebecca asked.

"Yeah. I'm going to lay back down."

"Come on, Mark."

As they left the driveway in Rebecca's car, Ready saw his old Toyota crumpled against the tree. He looked down at his feet and didn't look up again until they reached the highway.

Chapter 46

In a white cinder block room at the county jail, Will sat in an orange jumpsuit at a steel table that was bolted to the floor. His lawyer sat across from him. Beneath the harsh fluorescent light, Will looked much older than his fifty years.

"You're not going to beat this one, Will."

"Come on," said Will. "You're my advocate. You're supposed to be on my side."

"I *am* on your side. That's why I'm urging you to plead guilty."

"But I'll give you hundreds of hours of work between the trial and the appeal," Will said in a joking tone. "How can you turn down that kind of money?"

The lawyer leaned forward. "Will, I've worked with people like you before. You have a lot of money. You're used to getting what you want, and you think consequences are for other people. This time, you have to pay the consequences. You can't talk your way out of this, and you can't buy your way out.

"The police have *your* gun, with *your* fingerprints on it. There's a clear motive. Your wife hired him to see if you were having an affair. And you *were* having an affair. You killed the man in front of witnesses who have identified you. Before the shooting, you walked down the hall of a retirement home shouting repeatedly that you were going to kill him. You can't win this case, Will. You can't."

Will leaned back and nodded.

"Even if you could get past this," the lawyer continued, "there's still the smuggling. I've been talking with the team you hired for that case." He shook his head and frowned. "Your illegal worker gave the government a statement about the shipments he unpacked. But even if he hadn't, the Feds have enough other evidence to convict you. They found the fake passport in your desk. How do you think that looks? Why do you think you're locked up right now instead of being out on bail? They know you're a flight risk. And if you think the county prosecutor is aggressive on the murder charge, wait till you see how the Feds prosecute the smuggling case."

The lawyer leaned back and said, "Your other team wants to work on a plea deal on the smuggling charges."

"Why?" asked Will. "Why go down without a fight?"

"Because if you get convicted in either case, you'll be in prison for the rest of your life. The Feds will take back every penny you made from smuggling. They're going to seize your business. They'll make you pay for their investigation and for the prosecution if they can. Do you want to risk that? Do you really want to give up everything you've ever earned?"

"No," Will protested. "I don't want to give those fuckers anything. I'm not going down without a fight."

"Will, you're paying me to help you, and I'm trying to help you. You will lose, and you'll leave Susan with nothing. Is that what you want? Does Susan deserve that? You have the chance to avoid one last crime here, to spare one last victim."

Will took a deep, shuddering breath and looked down at the floor. The lawyer watched him in silence. After a few moments, without looking up, Will asked in a desperate, breaking voice, "Where is Susan? Where is she?"

"I don't know, Will. No one knows."

Chapter 47

In her sister's tiny Manhattan apartment, Ella spent most of her days asleep on the lumpy foldout couch with the springs that popped when she rolled over. At night, she listened to the traffic in the streets, remembering things she could not bring herself to talk about, while her sister slept peacefully in the next room with her boyfriend.

Anna, her ambitious, impatient, and perpetually over-caffeinated sister, had been unkind when she picked Ella up at JFK. "I had to borrow this car," she said. "You know I don't own a car. You can thank Jared when we get back."

Ella said nothing, and after several minutes of silence, Anna asked with undisguised annoyance, "Why are you so sullen? What the fuck happened to you? Why didn't you fly back earlier, on the first ticket I bought you?"

Ella turned away from the hostility she could not bear. She pushed her hair over the left side of her face to avoid her sister's gaze and looked out the window.

When they entered the apartment, Anna's boyfriend Jared was on the couch watching television, eating from a Chinese take-out box. He wore a business suit with the tie loosened and the collar open. He stood and shook her hand when Anna introduced them.

"Nice to finally meet you," he said.

Ella's hand was limp, and she said a weak hello before excusing herself to go to the bathroom. The rims of her eyes were red and her head ached. From the bathroom, she heard Jared ask, "Is she OK?"

"She just got what was coming to her," her sister said. "And now she has to grow up. Everyone knew this was coming."

"What happened?"

"I don't know," said Anna, her voice devoid of sympathy. "She won't talk."

Through the remainder of that summer, and into the first days of fall, Ella rarely left the apartment. When she did, she was overwhelmed by the bustle and noise of the street, and wanted only to crawl back into bed. Her lethargy and the cloud of gloom she brought to the apartment annoyed her sister. Sometimes just to get away from her, Anna slept at the noisy, dirty apartment Jared shared with two other men.

Anna tried to get Ella to go out, in hopes of getting her to open up and socialize. But when they were out, Ella was quiet and withdrawn, and she drank heavily. Hoping to drink herself to sleep, she often ended the night crying in public. Her exasperated sister could only yell at her to get her life together.

One night, Anna invited one of Jared's work friends to join them for drinks. He and Ella got drunk, and the next morning she awoke beside him on the foldout bed. She didn't remember having sex with him, but she overheard him say to Jared a few days later, "Oh, she's not all that. She looks nice, but in bed, she's a cold fish."

Ella didn't leave the apartment for four days after that.

Toward the end of September, Anna was going to work earlier and coming home later than Jared. In the mornings, Ella could feel Jared watching her from the little kitchen as she lay on the sofa bed. Whenever she showered and dressed in the tiny bathroom, he was sitting on the chair in the front room that had a view of the bathroom door. His eyes always seemed to catch her on the way out.

One morning, while she was still in bed, he sat down next to her with his cup of coffee and asked, "So what happened? How did you wind up in California?"

"Please don't sit on my bed," she said. Her back was to him, and she did not turn to face him.

"I'm just trying to help. You have to talk to someone."

She made no response.

He put his hand on her shoulder and rubbed it for a moment, then tried to roll her over.

"Get your hands off of me!" she shouted. She flung his hand away, and he spilled his coffee on the bed.

When Anna got home that evening and asked Ella about the stain, she told her what had happened.

"Oh, I don't believe that," Anna said. "You're making that up."

"I would never make up something like that. He's always looking at me, Anna. You have to get away from him. He's not right for you."

Anna's anger and resentment toward her sister exploded. "He does not look at you! You *wish* he would look at you! He told me you walk around the apartment in your underwear to provoke him."

"What? That's not true! I would never do that."

"Why would he lie, Ella? Why would he lie? That's exactly the kind of thing you'd do."

"No, Anna," Ella said, her voice weakening to a whimper. "I wouldn't."

"You're pathetic. And I'm sick of looking after you," Anna said bitterly. "I'm sick of seeing you mess up. You had talent in everything you ever tried, but you always walked away before it got too hard. Before you could fuck it up. You were a dancer, and a good one, until you quit. You were an A student, but you didn't go on to law school. Well, guess what, Ella? This is your life, and you fucked it up, and you can't just walk away this time.

"Whatever happened while you were slutting around California finally woke you up, didn't it? And what did you learn? That you just wasted the last three years of your life! And now you're going to have be a grown up, like me and everybody else. Don't you ever touch Jared, you fucking slut! I don't want you in this apartment anymore."

Anna slammed the door of her bedroom while Ella sobbed on the couch.

In her dreams that night, she kept catching glimpses of Ready among the crowds of the city. She ran and ran, but she couldn't find him.

Chapter 48

Ready's room in the rehab facility looked like a small college dorm room, with a narrow single bed, a small desk and chair, and a window overlooking a grassy field. Ready lay on his side facing the wall, running his fingers over the pale-yellow paint of the cinder blocks. He spent much of his free time studying the rough surface of this wall. The texture resembled an orange peel.

During this quiet time between meetings each afternoon, some variation of the same dialog ran through his mind.

Why did I choose to live? I don't know. I'll have to find out as I go.

Why did Susan let me into her world? I don't know. Did she have a choice?

Why did Ella latch onto me the way she did? I don't know.

Why did I latch on to her? She accepted me. She believed in me more than I believed in myself. And she was lovely. Everything in her was lovely. She made the world around her beautiful.

What did I see in her? The promise of happiness. Joy. Beauty. Love.

Did I believe in those things? I believed in her.

Where is she now? I don't know.

Where is Susan? I don't know.

Will I ever know? I don't know.

What are my triggers? The bar. The sight of the bottle, or of someone drinking. Stress and bad times. Happiness and good times.

Will life be just a dead level from now on? Will there be any joy? Who are you kidding? There was no joy in drinking. Not in those last few years. It was just an illusion I clung to.

So what will life be like going forward? Maybe the same as before, but without the confusion and poor judgment. Without the bed spins and the hangovers, the vomiting, the shame and self-hatred, and the nights I can't remember. That's already an improvement. Even if nothing else changes, the absence of those things means everything has changed.

What do I need to avoid? My whole former life. The bars, the people, the hours and days of doing nothing.

Which is the drink that will undo me? The first. That's the only one you have to say no to. Every day that you say no to that one, you win. And from here on out, life is a series of days. You must live each one with purpose, with attention, with presence, and mindfulness and gratitude.

Are you up to the challenge? Yes. I will always do my best. Always.

Where is Susan? God, I hope she's OK.

Where is Ella?

Ella, where are you?

Chapter 49

After the long drive to Palm Desert, Susan rested for three days and then traveled east to Saratoga Springs, New York, where she spent the next three months in the home of her last living relative, her father's sister in law.

She was happy to have the full breadth of the continent between herself and Will. They were separate people now, with separate fates. On some level, she had been mourning the death of the marriage for almost a year before she decided to hire a detective. Her grief had finally broken, like a fever, that night at Ready's, and with each passing week she felt a little better.

Her lawyer called every few days with news. Will's lawyer was pushing him toward a guilty plea on the murder charges. The federal government was close to indicting him on charges of smuggling, tax evasion, money laundering and distribution of counterfeit drugs. They would take from him every penny they could get. There would be little left for her when it was over.

She didn't care about any of this. She felt a mixture of pity and disgust for Will. He'd been a slave to his appetites and desires, and willfully blind to the suffering his selfishness had caused.

The only person she wanted to talk to was Ready, but she couldn't find him. Many nights, she dreamed they were walking together through dark woods, talking as they went, drawing closer until they were holding hands, neither one knowing where they were headed. They came upon a wall that marked the forest's end. He helped her over, and on the other side she found a place of warmth and light.

The first few times she had this dream, she felt such intense emotion upon entering into the light that she awoke immediately. In later weeks, as the dream repeated, she explored the new land.

Then the dream changed again. She would return to the wall to look for Ready, only to find he had never made it over. This version of the dream left her with an emotional hangover that lasted for days.

Ready never answered his phone, and eventually his number was cut off. Susan spent half an hour one day on Google Maps, trying to reconstruct the journey she had taken to the red-roofed house where she and Ready had made love. In a satellite view of Santa Barbara, she picked out what she thought was the house. She switched to street view and got the address. Then she wrote letters by hand and mailed them.

Warren,

I'm in Saratoga Springs, New York.

My parents brought me here for Thanksgiving when I five. The ground was white, the skies were grey, and the trees were bare. Coming from San Diego, I had never seen such a landscape. I cried for twenty minutes after we arrived. When my father asked me what was wrong, I asked why all the trees were dead. He said, "The leaves will come back in spring." I didn't know what that meant. How could something dead come back to life?

At night, when the soft snow crusted over and crunched beneath our feet, the sky was black and clear, and I saw more stars than I had ever seen before. I told my father that the more I looked, the more appeared. He said, "That's because your eyes are adjusting to the dark." I said, "No, it's because I'm looking harder. When they know how bad you want to see them, then they show themselves."

I asked him why there were so many stars, more than any person could ever count, and he said they were there so we would ask questions just like that, and so we'd know we were part of something bigger than the littered floor of suffering on which our lives play out.

I've been thinking a lot since I got here. Meditating, really. My marriage was a mistake. I took the wrong road, but somehow, it led me to the right place.

All my life, I was looking for a love that would never leave me. It was there all along, within me and around me, but in the darkness and confusion of my life, I couldn't see it. On this side of the wall, I see it in everything. I feel it everywhere. There is such a surfeit of love in me now, it overflows and could feed so many souls, but there is no one here to share it with.

I can't believe how lush this place is in summer. I can't believe these are the same dead trees that made me cry all those years ago. The only thing that troubles me now is the thought that you're still back there in the dark.

Warren, please call and let me know you're OK.

I'll find you when I go back. One way or another, I will. I want to bring you into this world you helped me find.

Love, Susan

Chapter 50

Ready left rehab after four weeks. Two weeks later, he stood next to Omar in an elevator. It was early October now, three months since Susan and Ella went away. Omar removed the panel of buttons next to the elevator door, and the two of them inspected the wiring.

"See, now, these go back to the main controller. On this type of elevator, just about the only time you ever have to pull this off is when one of the buttons breaks. You know, people get impatient and they start mashin' the buttons, and they crack."

Ready looked out the door of the elevator with a glum expression.

"Hey, man, you payin' attention?" Omar asked.

"No," said Ready.

"I'm tryin' to do you a favor here. If you learn this stuff and you pass the test, you can have yourself a decent job."

Ready looked morosely at the panel.

"Come on, man, how long did you last waitin' tables?" Omar asked.

"One day."

"You gotta get a real job. It's time to grow up. You ain't doin' yourself no favors by puttin' it off."

"I know," Ready said with a sigh.

"I'm tryin' to show you this shit, and you're acting like you just don't care."

"I hate to say it," Ready said, shaking his head sadly, "but I don't care. I don't really care about anything."

"Then get the fuck out of here, OK?" Omar snapped. "Go back to your boat and do whatever you do in there. I'm sick of wastin' my time on you."

Ready walked out of the elevator without saying a word.

Chapter 51

While Ready was walking away from Omar, Ella sat in a leather chair in an office in Manhattan. Behind a desk, a thin high-strung woman in her fifties examined a folder full of photographs. The only thing visible through the window behind her was another building, full of other people like her.

"Do you have anything more recent?" the woman asked.

"Those are only nine months old," Ella said.

"But you don't look like this anymore," the woman said. "You have a brightness in these photos. Like sunshine. I don't see that in you now. You look...eclipsed."

"I was out of modeling for a while," Ella said. "I went away."

"Your former agency told me you left without warning. They couldn't reach you. Did you run off after some man?"

Ella nodded.

"And he broke your heart," the woman said. "And now you need to support yourself again."

"There are kinder ways to tell that story," Ella said softly.

"But you don't have the same spunk you had here. You don't have that brightness in your eyes. You're not smiling." The woman closed the folder. "Look, you're a catalog model. You have that wholesome face that retailers like. You don't have the exotic edge that the fashion houses want. The best I can get you is more catalog work, but you have to smile. That sad face won't sell any bathing suits."

"I know."

"And you cannot run off on me. I want you to look me in the eye and tell me you won't run off."

"I won't," Ella said. "I'm done with all that."

"And you will always be reachable. When I call you, you will answer."

"I will," Ella said.

"OK. I'm sorry to be such a bitch. I want to take you on, but I don't want to get burned. How long have you been back in New York?"

"Almost three months."

"And is this the first agency you've contacted?"

"Yes," Ella said.

"What have you been doing for the past three months?"

"Recovering."

"From what? Did you have a drinking problem?"

"In a way."

The mention of drinking brought her mind back to the day she first saw Ready at her window and recognized him as a fellow traveller. Yesterday, when she'd been in a less troubled frame of mind, the memory had brought her joy. Today, all she could think of was how, in the misery of her captivity, she'd tried to dig her claws into him, like a falling cat grabbing at the last branch of a tree. Before the day was done, the memory would present itself a dozen more times, and each time, depending on her mood, she would see something different in it.

"You look pale," the agent said. "How can you be so pale after all the sun we've had?"

"I've always had fair skin," Ella said. "But I haven't been out in the past three months. And...yes, now I'm pale."

"Well, do yourself a favor and get outside. Go to the gym. Do *something*. Get some color back in your cheeks."

"I will," Ella said, as she stood to leave.

"I might have something for you in a week."

"Really?"

"In Hawaii. A catalog shoot. Four models. It's already arranged, but the blonde is a real bitch, and I'd like to send someone else, to teach her a lesson."

"Thank you," Ella said.

"I'll let you know in a couple of days."

Chapter 52

Ten days later, on a damp morning when the winds were cold and light, and a dark blanket of clouds hung over the marina, Rebecca appeared at the boat with a bag of groceries. Ready was on deck, cleaning the cabin windows with a dingy white rag.

"It looks good," Rebecca said.

"You and Gary going to take her out?" Ready asked.

"No. I don't think we could be confined to a boat right now. We'd kill each other. I brought you some food." She set the bag and her purse down on deck. "There's a lot of healthy stuff in there. Carrots, celery, things to make juice."

"Thank you," Ready said.

"I ran into your sponsor yesterday. He said you're having a tough time. I mean, not so much with staying clean. Just with life."

Ready shrugged. "It takes some getting used to, being sober all the time. My escape route is gone. I have to deal with everything head on."

"If you can actually do that," Rebecca said, "you'll be a lot better off than most people."

"And I have to deal with all the stuff I didn't deal with when I was drinking."

"Like what?"

"Like why did I treat myself so badly? What will I do with my life? How do I support myself without any skills? Things like that."

"Do you want to get off the boat?"

"Yeah. I'm trying different things. Nothing sticks."

Rebecca took a deep breath and said, "Mark, you have to get out of here. I'm sorry to have to tell you this, but Gary really wants you gone."

Ready twirled the cleaning rag and looked out to sea.

"Do you have anywhere to go?" Rebecca asked.

"No. Maybe my sister's."

"Where's she?"

"Seattle."

"I hope you like these clouds," Rebecca said, pointing toward the sky.

"I don't."

Rebecca's phone rang inside her purse. "Well you better get on it, Mark. Find a place to go. Promise me you'll keep in touch, and let me know if there's anything I can do."

"I will."

She dug around in her purse for the phone then finally dumped the whole bag out on deck. She picked up the phone from a pile of letters and said, "Hello?"

She listened for a moment then said, "I'm on the boat. I told you that's where I was going."

A breeze separated the letters and Ready collected them before they could blow into the water. One of the items in the pile was a postcard from Saratoga Springs addressed to Warren Lane.

"We're just talking, Gary. What's wrong with you?" Rebecca listened again for a moment. "No," she said. "No!" She paused again then said, "Fuck you!" and hung up.

Ready picked up the card and read it: "Warren, please call. I just want to know you're OK. Love, Susan." Her number was written underneath.

"God, he's such an ass sometimes," Rebecca said. She put down the phone and turned to Ready. "What are you looking at?"

"This card from Susan."

"Oh, the mysterious Susan," said Rebecca. "She sends letters to the house every week addressed to Warren Lane. I was collecting them to send back, but Gary got drunk the other night and opened them. We were having dinner with some friends, and Gary started reading them aloud, like they were funny. It almost made me cry. That poor woman loves that man so much, and he's dead. Did you know that? He was murdered. I don't know how she got our address. Imagine being in love with someone and not being able to find them." These words made Ready think of Ella.

"Imagine how that must hurt," Rebecca said. "And he's dead this whole time, and she doesn't even know it."

"But he's not dead!" Ready exclaimed. "And neither is she. She can't be!"

Startled by the intensity of his emotion, Rebecca asked, "What's the matter, Mark? Who is *she*?"

Without answering, Ready went below deck with the postcard. Rebecca called after him a few times, but he didn't respond. Finally, she sighed and said, "Call me if you want to talk." She moved the bag of groceries to the cabin entrance and left.

Chapter 53

Below deck, Ready studied the photo of the little town on the front of the postcard and the handwriting on the back. Then he turned on his phone and dialed the number.

"Hello?" Susan said.

"Hi, Susan."

"Warren? How are you? Where have you been? Are you OK?"

"I'm OK," Ready said. "How are you?"

"Better. Much better than I was a few months ago. Why did you tell me you were Warren Lane?"

"I wanted to help you."

"Well, you did. What's your real name?"

"Mark Ready."

"Blah! I'm going to call you Warren."

"You certainly *sound* better," Ready said.

"I want to see you."

"Where are you?" Ready asked.

"New York State. Saratoga Springs. It's beautiful here. The leaves are gold and red, and the air is crisp."

"What are you doing there?"

"I had to get out of town after the murder. But I'm coming back next week to meet with my lawyers. Will was involved in some bad business. Actually, Warren, I'll come sooner if I can see you. All I want to do right now is see you."

"I'd like to see you too."

"I'll book a flight," Susan said. "I'll call you back within the hour."

"OK," said Ready.

"I'm so glad to hear your voice. Wait for my call, OK? This is your phone, right?"

"Yeah."

"I love you, Warren."

"I love you too," Ready said sadly.

An hour later Susan called and said she would arrive the following evening. They agreed to meet for breakfast in two days at a restaurant near the marina.

Chapter 54

The evening before Ready and Susan were scheduled to meet, Omar walked down the dock carrying a brown paper bag. A cool autumn wind blew beneath the blackening sky, and the boats in the marina rocked gently to the sound of the tiny waves lapping at their hulls.

Omar found Ready's boat and descended into the cabin. Ready was stretched out on the bed, staring blankly at the ceiling.

"Nice boat," Omar said.

"Yeah." Ready's voice was emotionless and flat.

"You don't mind if I drink in front of you, do you?" Omar asked.

"No," said Ready.

Omar pulled a beer from the bag and said, "What do you drink if you can't have alcohol?"

"Juice."

"I used to drink that," Omar said. "When I was four. How you likin' it?"

"It's boring as hell. I never realized how much time there is in a day."

"What made you decide to clean up?"

Ready rolled a little to one side and rubbed his finger along the wall next to the bed, as if checking for dust. "I got sick of hating myself. And I wasn't ready to die."

"So what do you do all day?"

"Clean the boat. Take walks. Read. Think about Ella."

"The blonde you told me about?"

"Yeah, the blonde."

"Where'd she go?"

"I don't know."

"Why don't you find her?" Omar asked.

"I've tried," Ready said. "I've tried everything."

"You try calling her?"

"A thousand times. Her number doesn't even ring anymore."

"And she hasn't called you?" Omar asked.

"No. She might think I'm dead. You know, that whole shooting thing. And after I lost my phone, I bought one of those pay-as-you-go phones. It has a different number."

"Why didn't you get a new phone on your existing plan?"

"Because I'm a dumb-ass," Ready said with frustration. "And I was drunk for forty-five days and didn't pay my bill."

"Damn. You don't sound like the kind of man a woman wants to keep around. You sure she's interested in you?"

Ready sat up and said with desperation, "She has to be. Or...or what else is there?"

"Maybe she can look you up," Omar said.

Ready shook his head. "I never told her my real name."

"You just told her your name was Warren?"

"Yeah."

"All right," Omar continued, "what about email?"

"I don't know her email address."

"Facebook?"

"She doesn't use it," Ready said. "And I don't know her last name."

"You don't know her last name?" Omar asked.

"No."

"Dude, you're in love with this girl and you don't even know her last name?"

"Does that surprise you?" Ready asked.

Omar remembered their conversations in the sports bar. "Not really. You didn't even know your own name the first time I asked. How'd you meet her anyway?"

"She caught me peeping in her window."

"You were peeping in her window? What did she do when she caught you?"

Ready thought back to their first meeting, and some light finally showed in his eyes. "Well, um... she pulled down my pants and fucked me."

Omar nodded as he considered the scene. "Well," he said thoughtfully, "I could see why you would like a woman like that. She sounds very..." He searched for the right words. "Outgoing. And generous."

"She is," said Ready.

"I think you found a kindred spirit there," Omar said. "It sounds like she just looked at you and said *yes*, the same way you were always doing. Say yes and see what happens next." Omar took a sip of his beer. "If two people as open as that cross paths, how can they ever untangle themselves?"

"I knew who she was as soon as I saw her," Ready said, "and it terrified me."

"Who was she?"

"The person who was going to make me grow up. The funny thing is, I *wasn't* saying yes that day. I kept trying to say no. I wanted to leave, but she wouldn't let me go. And now all I want is to have her back."

The two were silent for a moment.

"Hey," said Omar. "Hold your head up, man. She's out there somewhere."

"But where? Where is she?"

"I don't know. But if there's anything I can do to help, I'll do it. Cause I don't like seein' you like this. A guy like you wasn't born to be mopin' around inside a boat all by himself."

"Thanks, Omar."

"Hey, you know what?" Omar said. "Your friend Susan's back in town."

"I know."

"I ran into her about an hour ago at the Canary."

"What were you doing there?"

"Elevator failed inspection. It was an easy fix. Dude, I think that woman loves you."

"She does."

"She asked me a million questions. She made me give her my number so I can spy on you and tell her what you're up to."

"What will your first report be?"

"That you're a sad-ass motherfucker."

Shortly after Omar left, Susan called to confirm their meeting. "Can you meet early?" she asked, "I'm still on East Coast time, and for the past week I've been really hungry in the mornings."

"Sure. I wake up at six these days."

"Can we meet at seven?"

"Seven is fine," Ready said. "I'll see you then."

Chapter 55

The next morning, when Ready walked from his boat to the café, Susan was waiting for him just outside the door. She hugged him and kissed his cheek. Her skin was radiant, like Ella's had been the first time he saw her.

She looked at him with soft eyes and an open spirit, not the measuring scrutiny he had come to associate with her, and she saw immediately that he was suffering.

"What's wrong?" she asked.

Ready shrugged. He sat on the bench outside the cafe and looked down at his feet.

"I saw your friend Omar at the hotel last night," Susan said. "He told me you were sad, but I didn't think it was this bad."

"What did Omar tell you?"

"That you're trying to find work. Or not trying, in his opinion. We swapped phone numbers. He's worried about you." Then she added, "I can't tell you how happy I am that I met you. You don't know how you changed my life."

Ready looked at her but said nothing.

"Are you OK, Warren?"

"My name is Mark," Ready said.

"I can't call you that. You're Warren to me." She paused a moment, then observed, "You look healthy. Your skin is clear and your eyes are clear, and your face is less puffy than it used to be."

"I quit drinking."

"I'm glad," she said. "It wasn't good for you." She put her hand on her belly and added, "I don't know how you put up with all those hangovers. It's awful to wake up nauseous every morning."

She searched his eyes, but she could see he didn't understand what she was trying to tell him. She sat by his side and said, "Warren, you were kind to me at a time in my life when I desperately needed kindness, and I will always be grateful to you for that. Why are you so sad?"

She stroked his hair and kissed his cheek, but he wouldn't look at her.

"What's the matter, Warren? Did a woman do this to you?"

When he finally turned his face to her, she saw a sorrow in his eyes that she knew was beyond her reach.

"Oh, Warren," she sighed. "I would do anything to see you happy."

Then, with some excitement, she said, "Why don't we go for a drive? Remember when I was sad, and you dragged me out of that hotel? It was good for me. We can eat later. Come on! What do you say? I'll drive."

Ready said nothing.

"Remember, all joy begins with..."

"All right," he said reluctantly.

As they drove up the highway toward Goleta, Susan said, "I was in upstate New York for months. My lawyer hustled me out of town right after the murder. That time away was really peaceful. My aunt gave me a lot of time to myself. I didn't think I could spend so much time alone without feeling lonely. But it was exactly what I needed."

Ready occasionally looked out the window toward the dry Eastern hills, but mostly he looked down at the floor. When she finished speaking he studied her face for a long time.

"You're staring at me," Susan said with a smile. "The way I used to stare at you."

"Remember when I came to your hotel room that first time?" Ready asked. "And you said I glowed?"

"I remember," Susan said.

"Now you have the glow," Ready said.

Susan pulled the car to the curb and Ready looked up to see the burnt-out shell of Ella's house.

"You know what's funny?" Susan said. "My lawyers say that of all Will's properties and accounts, this is one of the few I'll be able to salvage. The rest is going to the government and the lawyers."

She pointed to the house. "Will set up a trust that owned this house. He did it because he didn't want me to find his name attached to it in the public records."

Susan turned her eyes from the house to Ready. "He kept a woman here," she said, "and he didn't want me to find out about it. But I guess you knew all that. Funny, huh? He bought this place to carry on his affairs, and now it's one of the only things I'll have left from him."

Ready said nothing. She saw his eyes staring toward the house and his mind far, far away. She remembered his curious comment that first day at the hotel, when she asked him who her husband was sleeping with, and he replied, "She's a wonderful girl."

"Oh, Warren," she said. "Was it her? Was she the one who broke your heart?"

Ready looked at her sadly and then looked away.

"Does she love you too?"

"I don't know," Ready said. "She used to. But I can't find her. She disappeared the day the house burned down. I don't even know if she's alive."

"She must be, Warren. There were no bodies in the house."

"Take me home," Ready said.

"Warren..."

"Take me home. I don't want to be here anymore."

She drove him back to the marina and as he opened the door to leave, he stopped and said, "Do you remember that day at the hotel?"

"When you tried to rush me out of the room?"

"Yeah. I promised I would tell you who it was."

"It was her?"

"Yes."

Susan took a deep breath. "It's a good thing she didn't show up, Warren. That would have been bad."

"But she did show up," Ready said. "When you were kissing me. She was there in the doorway, watching. That's the last image I have of her, looking at me with that hurt in her eyes. I don't know if she'd ever take me back."

Ready left the car, and Susan watched him crawl into his boat like a hermit crab withdrawing into its shell.

Though the thought of him with Will's mistress turned her stomach, Susan's devotion to him was unyielding. She meant what she had said earlier, that she would do anything to see him happy—even if it meant relinquishing him to a woman she detested.

Chapter 56

When she returned to the hotel, Susan dug through the files Ready had given her from Will's computer and found a series of emails between Will and Ella Weyland. She looked up the name on the Internet, but found nothing. Browsing again through the files, she found one angry message from Ella to Will that was signed "Eleanor."

A search for Eleanor Weyland turned up a web page from a modeling agency in New York announcing Eleanor Weyland as the agency's newest addition. The page had been posted just a few days ago and promised that her portfolio would be available soon. Susan studied the lone photo of Ella. "She is pretty," she thought.

Susan went to the contact page and found the agency's phone number. She started to dial it, and then hung up. She went back to the computer and did a search for doctors in New York. Then she dialed the agency again. When a woman answered, Susan said, "I'm calling for Ella Weyland."

"I can put you through to her rep," the woman said. "Just a moment."

Another woman picked up and said, "This is Pat."

"Hi, I'm calling for Ella Weyland."

"Is this about an engagement?"

"No. This is doctor Meredith Bergman from Columbia University Medical Center. I need to speak to her about her lab results, and I can't reach her through the number we have on file."

"Oh. Hold on," said the rep. "Let me get you her number."

"Do you know where she is?" Susan asked.

"She's in Hawaii. They're just wrapping up a shoot."

"How long will she be there?"

"They finish today. After that, I don't know. She has a week before her next shoot. I don't know what her plans are. Do you want her number?"

"Yes, please."

Susan took down the number, thanked the woman, and hung up. Then she picked up the hotel phone, took a deep breath, and dialed.

The phone rang four times before someone answered. Expecting to hear the energy and assertiveness of the young woman in the video, Susan heard instead a shy and tentative "Hello?" Struck by the honey-smooth voice, Susan could say nothing.

"Hello?" Ella repeated.

"Ella?" Susan asked.

"Yes?"

There was a long silence as Susan tried to stop shaking and speak. Finally, she asked in a timid voice, "Where are you?"

"At the Halekulani. Who is this?"

"How long will you be there?" Susan's voice trembled.

After a brief silence, Ella asked again, "Who is this?" She waited a few seconds for an answer, but Susan couldn't bring herself to speak again, and Ella hung up.

Susan looked up the Halekulani's web site. "Nice place," she said, as she clicked through the photos. Then she went to Expedia and searched for plane tickets. She called Omar as she searched.

"Can you fly to Hawaii today?" she asked.

"What?" asked Omar.

"I want you to take Warren to Hawaii," she said. "Today. As soon as possible."

"Oh," Omar hesitated. "I don't know."

"Please do this for me, Omar. Do it for Warren."

Omar was silent.

"Just say yes," she said.

"OK," said Omar.

"I'm booking your flight now. What's your last name?"

"Ramos."

"Can you come directly to the hotel?"

"Yeah, sure. I'll be there in half an hour. What room?"

"414."

Susan met him at the door when he arrived. "Here are your boarding passes," she said. "Your flight leaves in two hours. This is the hotel you're going to." She handed him a page printed from the Internet. "It's all on my card. This is the woman you're looking for." She handed him a photo of Ella. "Make sure he finds her. Please do everything in your power to find her."

"Why don't you take him?" Omar asked.

"Oh, I..." she choked up. "I couldn't hand him over to her."

"So I'm supposed to tell him I'm taking him to Hawaii to meet this girl? This is the one he's been pining for, huh?"

"Don't tell him anything about the girl" Susan said. "I'm afraid if we get his hopes up and she's not there, the disappointment will be too much."

"What if he doesn't want to go with me?" Omar asked.

"This is Warren we're talking about. Ask him to follow you over a cliff, and he'll say, 'OK, yeah.'"

Omar shook his head. "He's not like that anymore. He doesn't want to do anything."

"Hold on a minute," she said.

She wrote a note on a piece of paper, folded it up, and handed it to him. "If you get stuck, read that to him."

"All right," Omar said.

"OK, now go," Susan said. "Hurry!"

Chapter 57

Lying in his bed in the cabin of the boat, Ready heard Omar's voice call from the deck above. "Come on, buddy. Today's the day."

"What day is it?" Ready asked.

"The day you say goodbye to this boat," Omar said as he entered the cabin. "We're goin' on a trip."

"Where are we going?" Ready asked.

"To Hawaii."

"What for?"

"What do you mean, what for? When did you start askin' questions?"

"I don't know."

Omar looked him in the eye and said, "Come on. I really want you to do this, man."

Ready stared back at him for a moment, not sure what to make of this earnest, direct appeal. He shrugged, "OK."

He put a change of clothes into his backpack, and in five minutes they were on their way to the airport. Ready complained that Omar drove too fast.

"We don't want to miss this flight," Omar said.

A short while later, as they passed through security, Ready grew anxious. "There are too many people here," he said.

"You don't like being around people?" Omar said.

Ready shook his head. "No."

"Just look down at the floor, man, and hold my hand. I'll take you to the gate."

Ready did as Omar asked, but when they reached the gate, Ready pulled back.

"What's the matter?" Omar asked.

"I have to go to the bathroom."

"Then go," Omar said.

Ready was still in the bathroom when the desk agent made her second call for all passengers to board. Omar went into the bathroom and yelled, "Yo, Warren!"

There was no response.

He walked down the row of stalls, looking under each of the closed doors. One door had no feet behind it.

Omar knocked and said, "Warren. Come on, we gotta get on this flight, man."

"I can't do it."

"Too many people?"

"Too much everything," Ready said. "I want to go back to my boat."

"No you don't."

"Yes I do," he said. "I don't want to see anyone and I don't want to do anything."

Omar heard the final boarding call come through the speakers. "Come on, we gotta go! Now!"

"No," said Ready.

Omar removed the folded note from his pocket. "I got a message for you here from Susan."

"From Susan?"

"Yeah. She says..." He held the note up and read it. "All joy begins with yes."

Ready opened the stall door and examined the note. "Did Susan ask you to do this?"

"Yeah."

"Why?"

"I don't know, buddy. Just get on the fuckin' plane, all right?"

Omar looked at him waiting for a reply. "What do you say?"

Ready looked again at the note. "Yes."

Omar grabbed his arm and pulled him to the gate, which the desk agent closed behind them.

As the plane taxied onto the runway, Omar said, "You know, I think this trip is already doin' me some good."

"How's that?" Ready asked.

"My girlfriend's pregnant, so I gotta work on my parenting skills. Haulin' your ass through a crowded airport is good practice. When you started freakin' out at security, and I had to hold your hand, I just kept sayin' to myself, 'See, you can do this Omar. You don't have to lose your temper and beat his face in. Just hold his hand and you'll get through it.'"

"I'm happy to be your teacher," Ready said.

"But let's get one thing straight right now," said Omar, pointing a warning finger at Ready as the takeoff pushed them back against their seats. "If you try to exit this plane during flight, I will beat the living shit out of you!"

Ready looked out the window and watched the city fall away beneath them. After a brief layover in Los Angeles, they both slept through the long flight to Honolulu.

Chapter 58

Susan spent the next few hours watching television, fidgeting, and checking the status of Ready's flight. When Omar texted her to say they'd landed, her anxiety increased.

As Omar and Ready climbed into their taxi at the airport, Ella was just getting into hers at the hotel. A few minutes later, Susan's concern for the success of the plan surpassed her fear of talking to Ella, and she called her directly from her own phone.

"Hello?" Ella said as her cab made its way down the street.

"Ella?"

"Who is this?" Ella demanded angrily.

"Susan Moore. Will's wife."

Ella was quiet for so long, Susan finally asked, "Are you still there?"

"What do you want from me?" Ella asked.

"I want you to go to the hotel pool."

"Why?"

"To meet Warren Lane."

"Warren's dead!" Ella shouted. She hung up.

She stared out the window of the cab. The camaraderie and diversion of work, the sea and warmth and open skies would all be behind her in a few hours. Ahead was the chill of autumn, the lengthening nights, concrete and noise, and the seething canyons of Manhattan.

She would return to the small apartment she shared with her sister and resume the silent labor of her grief, trying to stuff back into that broken heart the hurt it could not contain. The little bit of color the days of sun had put into her cheeks began to fade.

"You OK, Miss?" the driver asked. Ella looked up to see him watching her in the rear-view mirror.

"No," she whispered, and shook her head.

Her phone chimed, and she looked down to see a text from Susan: "You can't let it end at that room in the Canary, with him kissing another woman."

She stared at the message in bewilderment for a long time, until finally, overcome with curiosity, she called Susan. "How did you know about that?" Ella asked softly. "I never told anyone."

"Warren told me this morning," Susan said. She waited, but there was only silence at the other end. "Ella, the man my husband killed was not your Warren. Didn't you see the photos in the news?"

"No," Ella said in a flat, numb voice. "I left right away, and I never looked back. It was too painful." In a barely audible whisper, she added, "It was my fault. I provoked him."

"Ella, go back to the pool," Susan said. "I sent him there to find you. He's waiting for you. Please go claim him. Otherwise, he's just going to drift forever, like lost luggage. You know how he is."

"Look, I'm sorry for what I did with your husband," Ella said, her voice breaking with regret. "I truly am. But if this is your way of getting back at me, it's too cruel. You can't be that cruel." She hung up and looked out the window, struggling to regain control of her emotions.

She thought back again to the day she first met Ready. How helpless he seemed when she had teased him! She remembered how he had left her alone on the back of the boat, forcing her to learn how to sail on her own. She remembered how their physical and emotional responses to each other were so much stronger than their reason and their will.

Then Susan's words made her smile. He was adrift. He did need to be claimed. Susan must have known him to have chosen those words.

Then she wondered. *Could someone I so brazenly wronged really want to do me a favor? Or could anyone be so cruel as to send me out to that pool to wait for a love that would never return?*

Susan's question echoed in her mind. "Didn't you see the photos in the news?"

Ella took a deep breath and picked up the phone from her lap. The taxi carrying Ready and Omar passed her on its way to the hotel, but she didn't see it as she turned her eyes to the little screen. She typed into the search box "Warren Lane." The last word, "murder," appeared on its own, and she tapped the search button.

The first result was the news report she had heard that day in the juice bar. She tapped and listened again to the final words of her former life:

"A shooting in a downtown office late this morning left one man dead. The victim was identified as Warren Lane, a private detective. Witnesses say local business owner William Moore walked into Lane's office and shot him to death, apparently without provocation."

Then she saw the photo of the smug, green-eyed man and the caption at the bottom of the screen: *Warren Lane.*

In a breaking voice, she cried, "Turn around! Take me back!"

The driver lowered his head to look at her in the rear-view mirror. "You want to go back to the hotel?"

The cabbie swung the car around.

* * *

Omar received a text from Susan as his cab pulled into the hotel drive.

"Go directly to the pool. And let me know what happens."

Omar grabbed Ready's arm and said, "Come on, man, we're goin' to the pool."

"I didn't bring a bathing suit," Ready said.

"So, swim in your damn clothes," he said as pulled Ready through the hotel entrance.

"I thought you wanted to work on your parenting skills," Ready said.

"Sorry, man. It's just...I got a mission, and I don't want to fuck it up."

"What's your mission?"

"I can't tell you," Omar said. "But your mission is to follow me, and if I tell you to do somethin', you say..."

"Yes."

"That's my boy!"

* * *

Ella's cab pulled into the hotel drive just as Ready's left with a new set of passengers. She stepped out and walked slowly toward the entrance, leaving the cab door open behind her. In the fading distance, she heard the diver's voice calling. "Miss? Your bag! Miss?"

She picked up her pace as she passed through the lobby, her heart pounding with a mixture of anticipation and fear. What if he wasn't there? Would the disappointment break her? Would that be enough to send her over the edge once and for all?

Before she knew it, she was outside again, at the beachside pool, where the moist ocean air smelled of salt. As she scanned the crowd in silence, she felt as if she were in one of those recurring dreams where she would spot Ready in the crowd, and he would disappear before she could reach him.

Omar stood ten feet in front of her, looking from chair to chair in search of Ella. Ready stood a few feet off to Omar's right, turning slowly round to take in the scene about him. His anxiety began to rise in the great open space and the presence of so many people. As he turned toward the sea, Ella approached him silently from behind.

She reached for his shoulder, half-expecting him to disappear, as he always did in the dreams. But his flesh was firm beneath her fingers.

As he turned around, she feared she would see someone else's face.

But it was him, and he looked bewildered. He couldn't make sense of the face that was staring up at him. It was Ella, but it was not the bright young spirit he had known.

She examined him silently for a few seconds before saying his name. "Warren?"

"Ella?"

Omar turned at the sound of her name. "So this is the one," he said.

"I thought you were dead!" Ella blurted. "I thought you were dead, and I flew away, and I never wanted to go back there. My heart was broken! What happened? Where did you go? Warren, I missed you."

She hugged him, pressing her face hard against his chest, and clung to him tightly for a moment before pushing herself away to look at him again.

"What are you doing here?" she asked.

He stared at her dumbly while she studied him with Susan's wondering gaze. "I... I don't know," he stammered. His response brought the hint of a smile, and dawn broke upon her face like pale sun over a sodden country.

"I knew you would say that," she said, her smile broadening. "I can't tell you how much I missed you. I can't even begin to tell you."

"You don't have to," Ready said. "I felt the same way. Will you take me back?"

"Take you back?"

"I'm sorry I kissed that other woman in the hotel," Ready said. "I'm sorry." He couldn't bring himself to say what he thought she wanted to hear: that Susan didn't matter. Instead, he said, "I know it's hard to understand, but I couldn't have done anything differently."

Understanding that this was a part of his experience that didn't belong to her, Ella said in her simple, straightforward way, "It's OK, Warren. I'm sorry I got you shot to death."

"Oh," Ready shrugged. "That's all right. I needed it. The old me did. Did you know I quit drinking?"

"Really? You look healthier. How long has it been?"

"About seven weeks."

"That's not long."

"No," Ready said. "Remember that day you got mad about the cocaine? You stood outside the window of my car?"

"I've remembered it a thousand times," Ella said.

"I wasn't ready for you then. I still had a way to go before I hit bottom."

"I know."

"But when you disappeared, I worked really hard and I got there as fast as I could."

"Was it bad?" Ella asked.

"The bits I can remember," he said, thinking back on the little blue car smashed against the tree in Gary's driveway. "I think I did a year's worth of drinking in six weeks. Remember what you said that day? That you would give me everything?"

Ella nodded.

"Well, I'll give you everything, if you'll help me get my legs back under me. I still have a long way to go. Will you stand by me?"

"Of course. Yes." She paused, and for a moment the preceding months ran through her mind: her recklessness with Will, meeting Ready, losing him, her sister's hostility and judgment, her own regrets.

As Ready watched the memories play out across her face, he was struck again by how much she resembled Susan now—how those bright blue eyes now revealed a deeper inner life.

"I have a long way to go, too," she said. "I've done a lot of thinking in the past few months. Not all of it was healthy. I wish... I wish I could tell you everything I've gone through."

"Take your time," Ready said. "I'm not going anywhere."

Omar smiled as he watched them kiss.

"Have you been to the beach?" Ella asked.

"No," said Ready.

"It's beautiful. Come on," she said. "Let's walk."

Ready smiled and took her hand, and they walked onto the beach.

Omar made his way to the bar and ordered a beer. He called Susan and said, "We found her."

"How did it go?"

"About as well as it could go. Almost got me a little teary-eyed," Omar said.

"Oh, I'm so relieved. Thank you, Omar. Thank you so much."

Omar looked around again and said, "This is a hell of a place."

"You think your girlfriend would like it?"

"She'd never want to leave."

"I'll buy her a ticket."

"For real?"

"For real," Susan said.

* * *

Out on the beach, Ready said, "I have a confession to make."

"Yeah?"

"My name isn't really Warren."

"I know. What is your real name?"

"Mark," he said. "Mark Ready."

"Oh, that name doesn't suit you at all," Ella said. "You can only ever be Warren to me, and that's what I'm going to call you." She paused for a moment then said, "Now I have a confession to make."

"What?"

"My name isn't really Ella."

"It's not?" Ready asked with some surprise.

Ella shook her head. "Nope. It's Eleanor."

"Wow, I never would have guessed you were an Eleanor. That's a librarian's name. Can I still call you Ella?"

"Oh, yeah," she said with a smile. "That's what everybody calls me."

"What are you doing in Hawaii?" Ready asked.

"I was doing a shoot for a clothing catalog. We finished this morning. Now I'm just hanging out. What are you doing here?"

Ready thought for a moment. "I really don't know."

"How did you get here?" Ella asked with her teasing smile. "Do you know that?"

"This guy told me to get on a plane," Ready said. "I didn't want to. I was in the bathroom. But then he read me the note."

Ella watched him with a baffled expression before accepting that his answer couldn't make sense to anyone but himself. She thought for a moment, and then said, "Warren, I really think you should consider modeling. It's not like a normal job, where you have to sit at a computer all day or fix greasy machines. You just show up, they put a costume on you, and you try to look happy."

"I don't know," Ready said with a tone of doubt. "I'm not sure I have the brain power for that kind of work."

Ella laughed. "OK, just the fact that you said that—and meant it—tells me you'll do fine. I'll introduce you to my agent."

Chapter 59

Will took his lawyer's advice and pleaded guilty to all charges to avoid leaving Susan with nothing. Susan visited him only once in prison, where she spoke to him through a glass partition. His cheeks sagged beneath the dark circles that ringed his eyes. His skin was dry and pale, and his greying hair had grown brittle and thin. But his spirit was lighter than his grave appearance.

"The government isn't going to get any more out of me," he said. "The taxes are paid, the penalties are paid, the interest is paid. I even paid for part of their investigation. You know, it's not enough that they catch you. They have to insult you, too. But you have the house and the trust, and you should still get something from the account in New York."

"Martin says they can take some of that," Susan said.

"Some of the New York money," Will agreed. "But the money in the trust, that's all legit. Arnie and I were scrupulous about that. And that trust is as close to impregnable as the law will allow. They can't take anything from there. If Martin works with my lawyers, they should be able to set you up with enough to live on."

Will's smile was bittersweet. "It's funny, you know. I still get off on outsmarting those bastards, even though I'll never live to enjoy the money."

"You don't look well, Will. You look terrible."

"The doctor says my heart is failing." He shook his head. "And I'm not taking my medicine. I told the prosecutors I'd be out of here in six months, even if I have to leave in a casket."

He reflected for a moment. "I had my time," he said. "I had the money and the girls, the good food and wine. I travelled everywhere. That's more than most people ever get. I'm not going to rot away in this place for twenty years. Hey, uh…" Looking at her face, he patted his cheeks and smiled. "You put on a little weight."

Susan shrugged.

"It looks good. I always like to see you healthy." He smiled briefly, but the smile faded and two were quiet for a minute before Will resumed.

"I did my best to look out for you," he said. "Financially, anyway. I really did. Maybe you can't understand this after all the horrible things I've done, but I always did love you the best. You always were the most beautiful one to me. I'm sorry I couldn't be faithful. That's just not who I was. Sometimes I wish I'd never married you. That was the most selfish thing I ever did. I can't forgive myself for all the grief I caused you."

"Well, maybe it's like you said, Will. You couldn't be the faithful husband. That's not who you were. But something brought you to me. Something brought me to you. We had our life together."

"And this is where it ended," Will said sadly.

"This is where it ended," Susan said.

Chapter 60

True to his word, Will left prison in a casket within six months. Susan collected the insurance from the burned-out house and sold the lot where the house had stood. She sold the Santa Barbara house and bought a small cottage in Marin County. She gave up the proud façade that had inspired the admiration of her friends, and her new neighbors embraced her, as people are wont to do with those who wear their hearts open to the world.

On a warm October evening, a year after she'd sent Ready off to Hawaii, as the moon followed the evening star across the western sky, Susan sat on her patio talking and laughing with a neighbor over a glass of wine.

"So, is he really going to call?" her neighbor asked. She was tipsy and a little giddy.

"In just a minute, Jennifer," Susan said. "Or maybe a few. He's never on time."

"When's the last time you talked to him?"

"It's been a few months," Susan said. "And never on Skype. I haven't seen his face in a year. I mean, outside of a magazine."

"You seem nervous," said Jennifer.

"I am," Susan said. "I know why he's calling. I've been avoiding this."

"Does he really look like that?" Jennifer asked, holding up a magazine photo of Ready in a suit.

Susan laughed and said, "No. That's not him at all. I mean, the face, yes. But he would never wear a suit. I don't think he even knows how to put one on."

Susan stood up and said, "I have to go to the bathroom. If the call comes in, will you answer it?"

"Sure."

A minute later, Skype chimed on the iPad that Susan had propped on the patio table. Jennifer knelt by the table and answered the call.

"Hello?" she said. "Are you Warren?"

Ready looked confused. "Yeah, um, wait. Is Susan there?"

"She's here. She'll be back in a minute."

"Who are you?" Ready asked.

"Jennifer. A neighbor. I just dropped by for a glass of wine. Or three."

"Well, it's nice to meet you, Jennifer. I'm Warren."

"I know," she said, holding the up the magazine ad for him to see. "I didn't believe Susan when she said she knew you. I thought she was just collecting pictures of her crush."

Ready laughed. "Is Susan making friends up there?"

"Oh my God, she's like, the confidant of the entire neighborhood. Everyone talks to her."

"She's a good person to talk to," Ready said. "She's very wise."

"Wise indeed," said Jennifer, her words a little slurred from the wine. "Here she is." Jennifer took a seat to the right of the iPad, just out of Ready's view, and poured herself another glass of wine.

"Hi, Susan," said Ready.

Susan sat and studied him for a moment before responding. "Hi, Warren. It's nice to see your face after all this time. You look good. You look really good."

"Thanks. You look... you look a little tired."

Susan laughed. "You know how to flatter a woman, don't you?"

"Sorry, I just..."

"No need to be sorry," Susan said. "I *am* a little tired. I don't sleep enough. How's Miami?"

"Good," said Ready. "I think we found our place. I like the sea. Ella likes the sun."

"I'm happy for you both," Susan said.

For a long moment, neither one spoke. Then Ready said, "I sent you an invitation to our wedding."

"I know," Susan said. "It's been sitting on the kitchen table for weeks."

"Well?" he asked. "Are you coming?"

Susan looked down at her lap and was quiet for a moment. Then she looked at him and said, "Warren, the return address on the back of the envelope is in Ella's handwriting. My address on the front is in your handwriting. Does she know you sent that invitation?"

"Well, yeah," Ready said with some hesitation. "I told her."

"Before you sent it, or after?"

Ready paused for a second. "After."

Susan thought for a moment about the envelope. She recognized the broad, looping script on the back from the note Ready had given her in the hotel room all those months ago, when he had said with such pride, "My assistant wrote that."

"I didn't want her to find my response in the mail if she didn't know you invited me," Susan said. "That would be a rude surprise. If you're going to be married, Warren, you need to start thinking about things like that."

"I know," said Ready, looking like a sheepish schoolboy. "Ella reminds me about stuff like that all the time."

"She's training you," Susan said, then added with a laugh, "and you need it."

"I'm making progress," Ready said.

"Did you tell her we were lovers?" Susan asked.

"What?" exclaimed Jennifer from her chair next to Susan. Susan ignored her.

"Yeah, I told her," Ready said.

"How'd she take it?"

Ready shrugged. "Um... it took her a little while, but I think she accepted it with a lot of grace. She's tough. She really is. And she's an accepting person. And that was a weird, crazy time for all of us. It's all in the past now anyway."

"And we should leave it there," Susan said. "I really don't think I should come. It would just be awkward."

"But I want everyone to get past that," Ready said. "There are only a few people in the world who really matter to me. You're one. She's one. And this is our wedding. I want you there." He paused for a moment. "Are you still mad at her? Do you hate her?"

"I don't hate her, Warren. I'm not even mad at her. Anyone who's good to you is a friend of mine. But she must be scared of me. She had an affair with my husband."

"Wait, what?" asked Jennifer.

"Shhh," said Susan to Jennifer.

"She is a little scared of you," Ready said. "But I want you two to meet. I like to have everything out in the open. You both mean a lot to me. You have to be able to get along."

Susan pushed herself up and back in her chair, as if trying to move away from the screen. "It's not a good time for me to be travelling," she said. "I have a lot going on."

"You can't get away from work?"

"It's not that," said Susan.

"You have a new boyfriend?" Ready asked.

"No. No more men. Not for now, anyway."

"Then what? What's your excuse?"

Susan sighed and turned away and said, "Oh... I've been so bad, Warren. I keep meaning to tell you, but...." She picked at one of her fingernails and wouldn't look at the screen. "I wanted to let you go."

"Whatever you keep meaning to tell me, you can tell me when you get down here. Come on, Susan," he teased. "I won't take no for an answer. You have to come."

Susan shook her head. "I'm sorry, Warren, but no. It wouldn't be right."

Ready stared at her for several seconds in disappointment. "That really hurts, Susan."

"I know," she said sadly. "It hurts me too. But I need to see you. Maybe some time after the wedding? Do you think you'll be in California again?"

"I'll probably be out there in a few months."

"I promise I'll see you then," Susan said. "Will you promise to see me?"

"OK," said Ready with resignation. "I'll see you then."

After ending the call, Susan looked up at the bright star hovering above the horizon and was silent for a long time. Jennifer watched her the way Will once had, wondering where she went in those quiet moments when so much activity appeared behind the surface of her dark brown eyes.

Susan thought back to her first meeting with Ready in the coffee shop. How quickly she had judged him! She remembered her surprise at his first kiss, and how she tempted him later when she answered the door wearing only a towel. She remembered the hike in the mountains, the desperate morning in front of the pharmacy, and the drive to the red-roofed house beneath the palms. She remembered his words in the bathroom, the robe she took off for him, and how natural and right, absolutely right, was his touch and their being together.

"Did you know the evening star and the morning star are the same thing?" Susan asked, still looking up at the sky.

"No," said Jennifer.

"It's just a question of where it appears. When it rises in the east, it's the morning star. In the west, it's the evening star. It's not even a star, really. It's Venus."

Susan watched the planet for a few more seconds, then turned to her friend and said, "Venus was the goddess of love. There's a scene in *The Aeneid* where Aeneas is wandering on the coast of North Africa. The storms have blown him to this foreign shore, and he doesn't know where he is, or what he's doing, or where he's going. He's just lost.

"And Venus, his mother, watches him from above, and she takes pity on him. She comes down to Africa, and appears before him in the form of a simple shepherd girl, and she tells him where to go. He doesn't know who she is. But he's so lost and so desperate for direction, he follows her advice. And that's what sets him on his path. He makes his way to Italy, and founds a whole new country.

"In the ancient stories, the lives of the gods and the people were always intertwined. You don't see that in stories anymore. But what happened to Aeneas on that shore happens all the time. Someone catches you at the right time in your life. Somehow they say the right thing. Just a few simple words, and they set you back on your path."

She looked at Jennifer with a curious expression and asked, "Do they know? When people say these things, do they know their words are more than just words?"

"I don't know," said Jennifer. "I don't really think about things like that."

"I'm excited to see him," Susan said, thinking of Ready again. Then, as if speaking to no one, she repeated the words he had spoken a few minutes before. "There are only a few people in the world who really matter to me. You're one. And I want you to know…" She looked down into the stroller by her side and traced his features in the faces of the sleeping twins. "…before you walk away again, and go back to your life with her."

Acknowledgements

Thanks to Kristin Mehus-Roe and Ingrid Emerick at Girl Friday Productions for their help in editing this book. Thanks to my beautiful and multi-talented wife, Lindsay Heider Diamond, for the cover design and interior design. You can find more of her work at http://www.lindsayheider.com. Thanks also to Camil Tulcan for giving us permission to use the bottle cap image. You can find more of Camil's photos at https://www.flickr.com/people/camil_t/.

About the Author

Andrew Diamond lives in Charlottesville, Virginia with his wife and children. By day, he helps build digital repositories for libraries and universities. When he has time, he blogs at https://adiamond.me. You can contact him at andrew@adiamond.me.